"It's just a scrape. I'll wash up when we're done."

She gave him a quick smile, dirt still speckling her cheeks, loose tendrils of damp hair hanging around her face.

In that moment he remembered the Heather he used to hang out with. The Heather who used to race madly around the barrels he and Lee set up. The Heather who would help build tree forts and go riding out in the hills.

The Heather he had so easily fallen in love with. He felt a resurgence of the old yearning she could create in him, a crack in the defenses he had spent so long building up against her.

He spun away, irritated with himself and his reaction. He was supposed to be immune to her. Years ago, Heather had chosen Mitch and a lifestyle that had taken her far away from Refuge Ranch. Far away from him. They were on completely different paths now.

Yet, even as his words kept time with his pounding heart, he couldn't stop another glance back at her over his shoulder.

Carolyne Aarsen and her husband, Richard, live on a small ranch in northern Alberta, where they have raised four children and numerous foster children and are still raising cattle. Carolyne crafts her stories in an office with a large west-facing window, through which she can watch the changing seasons while struggling to make her words obey.

Books by Carolyne Aarsen

Love Inspired

Visit the Author Profile page at Harlequin.com for more titles

Reunited with the Cowboy

Carolyne Aarsen

HARLEQUIN® LOVE INSPIRED®

Recycling programs for this product may not exist in your area.

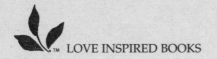

ISBN-13: 978-0-373-87950-2

Reunited with the Cowboy

Copyright © 2015 by Carolyne Aarsen

www.Harlequin.com

Printed in U.S.A.

See, I have engraved you in the palms
of my hands. Your walls are ever before me.
—*Isaiah* 49:16

For Lula Gelderman, faithful and steadfast.

Chapter One

She saw the truck a split second too late.

The snow swirling up from her tires and the sun shining directly in her eyes blinded Heather Bannister as she crested the hill. The pickup was coming right at her and there was nowhere to go.

So she did what any self-respecting country girl would.

She swerved, then stepped on the gas.

The back end of her car fishtailed on the icy patches of gravel as she fought to get it away from the truck, praying her tires would grab something. Anything.

She caught a glimpse of a panicked face behind the wheel of the pickup as her tires spun on the road. A half second before she would have been hit, she gained enough traction to move her car past the vehicle, missing it by mere inches.

And sending her directly toward the ditch. This time Heather slammed her foot on the brake and madly turned the steering wheel.

But with a crash and a heavy thud, the side of her car slammed into the bank of old spring snow. The impact spun her around, so that the front of her vehicle plowed into the bank.

Dazed and confused, Heather sat without moving for a moment, the whine of her engine and the ringing in her ears the only sounds she heard.

A heavy ache radiated from her shoulder, across her chest and up her neck, surprising in its intensity. For a stunned moment Heather wondered if the airbag had even done its job, but it lay deflated across her lap, proof that it had, in fact, deployed.

Hands still clenched around the steering wheel, she sucked in another breath and coughed on an exhalation. Her arms shook and her legs felt suddenly rubbery.

She had come within inches of a serious accident.

Her heartbeat thundered in her ears as reaction set in. Her legs were trembling now, adrenaline being replaced by a chill coursing through her body as her mind called up images of twisted steel and horrible injuries.

She shook the thoughts off. She couldn't allow herself to think of what-ifs. She hadn't hit the truck head-on. She had avoided a collision that would have had far worse consequences.

As she laid her head back on the headrest, trying to pull herself together, tattered prayers fluttered through her mind.

Thank You, Lord. Forgive me, Lord.

The same feeble petitions she had sent heavenward for the past few years. That was all she'd been capable of in the aftermath of the mess that was her married life with her ex-husband, Mitch.

An insistent banging on her door made her jump, adding to the piercing pain in Heather's head.

"You okay in there?"

The muffled voice outside the car and the continued thumping made her wince again as she painstakingly found the clip for the seat belt, then released it. But when she tried to open the door, it wouldn't budge.

She didn't need this, she thought, allowing herself a moment of self-pity. Stuck in the ditch only five miles from home, with a cell phone that was out of juice and some stranger banging on the window.

Then she pulled herself together. City life may have softened her, her ex-husband may have tried to beat her down, but this wasn't her first rodeo. She was Montana born and bred, and had once been a championship barrel racer. She had been thrown off horses, chased by ornery cows and she'd raced across rodeo arenas on an out-of-control horse. As her father always said, you can take the girl out of the country but you can't take the country out of the girl.

So she took a deep breath, turned in her seat, lifted her booted foot and gave the door a mighty kick.

Heather wished she had her sturdy riding boots on instead of these flimsy, high-heeled ones. But she created an opening and, grabbing her purse, slithered through it.

Her first step was onto the icy snow, and she would have stumbled forward had not the man outside her car caught her by the arm.

She found her balance, then looked up at her would-be rescuer.

And her heart plunged.

John Argall.

Son of the Bannisters' foreman and the man she had broken up with to move to New York. One of the people she had most dreaded seeing on her return to Refuge Ranch.

His blue eyes, fringed by thick lashes, stared down at her. "Hello, stranger," he said, but his voice, usually warm and friendly, was as cold as the snow under her feet.

Not that she blamed him. She was the one who had broken up with him. Who had ignored his warnings about Mitch and his big plans. Heather could have saved herself a world of hurt and regret had she listened to him. Had she not impulsively chased after what she'd thought would solve her problem.

Just like her biological mother always did.

"Hello, John," was all Heather could say, pushing the traitorous thought back. She hadn't returned to Refuge Ranch to indulge in might-have-beens. She was here only to help plan a bridal shower for her sister, Keira—an event Heather wouldn't be able to attend. She was off to Seattle to interview for an important job. A step in a new direction. Her debts were finally paid, her obligations fulfilled and she was ready to start a future on her own, free from any ties or romantic entanglements. She had made enough bad decisions the past few years; she was ready to look ahead.

"Are you okay?"

"I'm fine. Better than my car."

"Good to know, but you're right about your vehicle." He turned back to her car, buried up to the hood in the snowdrift. "Why don't you get into my truck and warm up while I find a tow rope?"

"I can help," she said, lifting her chin, her tone holding a defiant edge. Anger had been her defense the past few years; she deployed it now.

His eyes grazed over her knee-high boots, short skirt and thin wool jacket with its pleats and tiny buttons. She knew the designer clothes were more suited for the fashion runway than Montana spring weather, but they were the only type of clothes she had after years of living in New York. "You'll just fall in those heels," he said, with a deprecating tone that stung. "Besides, I wouldn't mind if you would check on my daughter, Adana. She's in the truck all by herself."

Heather couldn't stop the clench in her stomach as she looked back at John's truck, parked to one side of the road. The engine was still running, exhaust wreathing around the cab. Through the fogged-up window she could see a little girl sitting in a car seat. From the occasional notes and texts from her family, she had heard about John's marriage to her old friend Sandy, and the birth of his little girl, two years ago, two days before Sandy died of internal hemorrhaging.

The toddler's head bounced back and forth, the bright pink pom-pom on her winter hat bobbing with each movement, as if she was dancing in her seat. She waved mittened hands as she caught John and Heather looking at her.

John's daughter. Sandy's little girl.

Heather swallowed down her apprehension, then gave him a cautious smile, buying herself a few more moments. "By the way, I never had a chance to tell you that I was sorry to hear about Sandy's death. I know it was almost two years ago, but…well…I'm still sorry. It must have been hard for you."

John just looked at her, his expression unchanging. If anything, the set of his jaw seemed more grim. "Yeah. It was, but like you said, it was a while ago. We're coping."

His harsh tone cut, but Heather knew she didn't deserve anything more. She should have written or called. Sandy had been a dear friend to her, but she'd been dealing with her own problems at the time. Still, in spite of Heather's history with John, she'd known she'd owed her childhood friend the courtesy of sending him a sympathy card.

"Sandy was a good person, and at one time, a good friend," she said quietly.

His only reply was a tight nod, which made her feel even worse.

So she turned away, taking a careful step, trying to find her footing on melting snow. She faltered, almost losing her balance again, but John caught her.

Even through the thickness of her coat, she felt the solid grip of his hand on his arm, steadying her.

"You sure you didn't get hurt?"

"I'm okay," she said, surprised at her reaction to his touch. She pulled away, but then almost fell, her arms flailing as she struggled to regain her balance.

"Always were too stubborn for your own good,"

John muttered, catching her again and helping her to the road.

Heather shot him an annoyed glance, but didn't pull away until she found her footing on the gravel road.

"Go warm up," he said, pointing to the truck. "I'll need to attach a tow rope."

Six years ago she would have teased him about being so bossy. But that was when they were dating. When the foolish decisions Heather would make would result in a gentle reprimand from him and a smart remark from her.

Instead, she wrapped her coat around her, ducked her head against the gust of wind that had started up, and walked to the truck. She slipped a couple times on ice patches, unable to get the proper purchase in her high-heeled boots, but she finally made it. As she pulled open the door, cheerful music, Adana's happy chatter and blessed heat washed over her.

She climbed into the raised cab and pulled the door closed behind her, shivering as she turned to Adana, who was sitting in her car seat on the passenger side.

The little girl grew suddenly silent and stared back at her, eyes as blue as John's, curls of blond hair sticking out from under her winter hat.

Adana had John's eyes, his arching eyebrows. But she had her mother's delicate nose and generous smile. An ache settled in Heather's stomach as she looked at a child who was the same age as her own child would have been.

Six years they'd been apart, six years since she'd broken up with him, left Montana and him for Mitch and the high life of working as a model in New York City, and she could still make him feel like an idiotic teenager.

John yanked open the jockey box in the bed of his truck, the lid obscuring the occupants of the cab. He paused a moment, gloved hands resting on the edge of the box, trying to get his bearings. He'd known Heather was coming. Her arrival was all her adoptive parents, Monty and Ellen Bannister, could talk about. Every time he'd picked up Adana from the main house, where she spent time while he worked, he heard Keira and her mother laughing and talking about the bridal shower Heather would help them plan.

He thought he'd been prepared, but facing the reality of Heather was harder to deal with than the idea of her.

She had always been a stunning beauty, back when they'd dated. But now her face was narrower, her cheekbones more pronounced, her green eyes more wary, her hair even longer than when she'd left. Her expensive clothes were a far cry from the Wrangler jeans she used to favor. Altogether, they combined to give her an elusive beauty that had sucked the breath right out of him when she'd squeezed out of that car.

John pulled the coiled rope out of the box, his hands still trembling from the rush of adrenaline after almost hitting her with his truck, then seeing her again.

Though her car was buried nose deep in the ditch, Heather seemed unhurt. As for the other reason his heart was still pounding, well, she hadn't been a part of his life for a long, long time. When she broke up with him, he'd thought he was over her.

Guess not.

Her timing wasn't the best, though.

To the Bannisters, Heather was their adopted daughter, a wounded soul who needed extra protection. To him, she was a huge complication in the plans he'd been putting into place for the past few months. He just hoped her presence wouldn't jeopardize his business dealings with Monty, Heather's father.

Buying into a partnership on Refuge Ranch with Monty Bannister, his father's old boss, was all John had ever wanted since he was a young boy growing up there. Now, after months of methodical plans, calculations and deliberations, he had brought a solid proposal to Monty, just last week. He'd hoped the rancher would make a decision before Heather came home.

She could prove to be an unwelcome distraction. John knew Monty and Ellen hadn't been crazy about him dating Heather when they were in high school. He had always suspected that was the reason they'd encouraged her to go to college. Which had resulted in their breakup.

Just bide your time, he told himself as he slammed the lid of the toolbox. *Heather will be gone soon and Monty will give you his answer.*

John grabbed a shovel as well, then stepped onto his truck's bumper and dropped to the road. He started to dig up the snow Heather's car was buried in, taking his frustration with his unwelcome reaction to her out on it.

Ten minutes later he had to concede defeat. The

spring snow was hard, packed and icy. There was no way he was getting the car out on his own. There had been damage done to the wheels.

He found the tow truck number in his cell phone and dialed. Dwayne answered on the first ring.

"Yeah, I got a car in the ditch up here on the road to Refuge Ranch," John said as he walked to his truck. "Can you come and pull it out?"

"I'm actually right at Keith McCauley's place delivering an old truck," Dwayne told him. "I can be there in fifteen."

"We'll wait." He ended the call, then opened the truck door, and heard Adana chattering away.

"Pwetty earring. Like your earrings. I have earrings." She showed Heather the piercings in her ears that Sandy's mother had gotten for her last month.

But Heather, still sitting in the driver's seat, wasn't looking at his daughter.

"Do you need me?" she asked, clambering out of the cab, as if grateful for the distraction. She almost slipped on the ice yet again in her hurry to get away from the vehicle.

He was about to steady her again, but she found her balance, pulling away from his outstretched hand.

"I can't budge your car out of the snow, and one of the tires is popped off its rim. I've called Dwayne to pull it out. We may as well wait in the truck till he comes."

Heather folded her arms over her chest. "Sure. Okay." With a tight nod she climbed back into the truck, then moved over, closer to Adana, so he could swing in beside her.

It was a little too close for comfort, he thought, as he shut the door. *You'll have to help me through this, Lord*, he prayed as he turned up the fan in the truck. *Help me remember that Adana is my priority. Help me to remember Sandy and my promise to her to keep our daughter safe. Help me not to be distracted by Heather and her crazy life.*

It had happened too many times in the past. He hoped by now he had learned his lesson. Heather was like candy. Sweet, attractive, but with no stay-ing power. And as he glanced over at his daughter, he caught her watching him with her bright blue eyes, so like Sandy's it made his heart ache. Adana was his responsibility and she was all he needed in his life.

He felt Heather's arm brush his as she settled into the seat, her arms crossed, eyes resolutely ahead.

She couldn't look more uncomfortable if she was on her way to an execution.

He shifted closer to the door, reminding himself that Heather was a complication he just had to deal with until she was gone. Because she would leave. In spite of how excited her sister and mother were about her returning home, he knew she wouldn't stay as long as they believed she would. Leaving had been the story of her life and the refrain of their relation-ship. She couldn't have changed much in six years.

Chapter Two

Heather tried not to panic as she stood on the road watching her car, resting on the flat deck of Dwayne's tow truck, head back to Saddlebank.

It'll be okay, she reminded herself. How damaged could a car get from hitting a ditch? She chose not to think about the whine she'd been hearing since Rapid City, South Dakota. The car would be fine.

She was staying at the ranch until the weekend. That should give them enough time to fix it. Then she could head out to Seattle for her job interview.

A prayer hovered on the periphery of her thoughts, a remnant of a youth spent going to church. But she brushed it aside. She'd sent out many prayers the past few years. None of them had been answered, and she doubted any would be now. She had learned the hard way that she was on her own in this world.

A quick glance back showed her that John had already moved Adana's car seat to the middle of the cab, putting the little girl between the two adults.

As Heather got back in the truck, Adana reached out to her dad. "We see Grammy?" she asked.

"No, honey. We'll see Grammy another time," John said as he started the engine and made a U-turn on the road.

"Wanna see Grammy," Adana whined. "See Grammy."

"Sorry, honey." He gave Heather an apologetic look. "We were on our way to Sandy's parents for dinner. They're leaving on a trip and had hoped to see Adana before they went."

Heather felt guilty. She remembered all too well the first time Sandy, taking pity on the new girl at school, had taken her home with her. Kim Panko, Sandy's mother, had been friendly enough, but Heather had an innate ability to read people—a necessary skill developed as a result of the constant moves she and her natural mother, Beryl Winson, had made the first ten years of Heather's life. Over the course of the two girls' friendship, Sandy's mother had reminded Heather often how fortunate she'd been to be taken in and adopted by the Bannister family. She suspected Kim wouldn't be pleased to find out her return to Saddlebank was the reason John and Adana hadn't come for supper.

"I could have called my dad to pick me up," she said. "Or Keira."

"And it would have taken them half an hour to get here. It's fine."

Heather folded her hands in her lap, looking directly ahead, wondering if waiting in the chilly wind would have been preferable to riding with John and his daughter, feeling guilty because her mistake had prevented them from visiting Sandy's parents.

"Your mother is excited to see you," John said, his own eyes on the road. "That's all she's been talking about since she found out you were coming."

"I'm excited to see her and Dad, too. It's been so long."

"So why—" John stopped himself there. "Sorry. None of my business."

"Why was I gone so long?" Heather blamed the sharp note in her voice on the delayed reaction to plowing her car into the ditch. It had nothing to do with seeing her old boyfriend again.

John gave her a direct look, his blue eyes seeming to bore into her. Then he glanced away.

"I couldn't get the time off. I would have come if I could." The words sounded lame, even to her.

"Pwease, have earrings," Adana said, reaching for the feather-shaped baubles tangled in Heather's long hair.

"Those are too dangerous for you to play with," she replied.

"And probably too expensive," John added. He was smiling, but Heather caught the faintest hint of reproach.

She could have told him that she'd picked these up on the cheap from a street vendor at Herald Square as she'd been hurrying to an interview for yet another low-paying job. But saying so would require an explanation as to why she was forced to work in a retail job—any job, actually—when she'd made so much money modeling. Which would mean delving into the sorry state of her finances and her relationship with Mitch.

Your new job is the start of your new life, she reminded herself. *Only if you can get to Seattle. Only if your car gets fixed in time.*

Adana yawned loudly, then laid her head back against her car seat, blinking slowly. She looked tired, but turned to Heather again, softly smiling and reaching out to touch her arm.

Sorrow lacerated Heather's soul at the contact, and she felt as if her breath was sucked out of her body. Seeing this little girl up close brought back painful memories of her own loss.

"Are you sure you're okay?" John asked her. "You look like you're in pain. Did you get hurt when your car hit the ditch?"

Heather fought for composure, slowly breathing in and out. "No. I'm fine." The aches in her body would go away. The one in her soul would be with her always. She'd thought she had buried it, but Adana was a reminder of what she had lost.

"I hope she sleeps a bit," John was saying. "She's been out of sorts the last few days. Getting shuffled around too much."

"My mom takes care of her when you're working, doesn't she?"

"She did. But after your mom broke her neck, your mom's friend Alice has been helping out. She's a good person, just…" John stopped there.

"Not the same as her mother," Heather finished for him.

He nodded at her comment. "No. And I can't give Adana that."

Heather heard the sorrow in his voice and felt a glimmer of envy for the person he was grieving.

"Your daughter looks a lot like Sandy," she couldn't help saying.

"That's what everyone tells me," John replied, his features softening as he smiled at his little girl. "Thankfully, she has Sandy's sweet personality, too."

"Lucky her. Sandy was a wonderful person and a good friend. I'm sure…I'm sure you miss her."

John laid his hand on Adana's legs, curling his fingers around them, as if reinforcing the connection between them. "Thankfully, I still have Adana."

Heather knew his comment was a simple statement of fact, but she couldn't help feeling a gentle reprimand. She should have sent a sympathy card after Sandy's death, but Heather and John had had a complicated history. Too many missed opportunities.

Too many wrong choices.

Heather stopped herself from delving into the past as she stared at the road ahead. This visit to the ranch was a chance to catch her breath. Connect with her family before she headed out to a job that she felt would give her some control over her runaway life.

She glanced at John's profile. In spite of the tension that seemed to have settled between them like a silent visitor, she felt that curious twinge of attraction that was always between them.

His features were even, well proportioned. His narrow nose, angled cheekbones and strong chin with the faintest hint of scruff all combined in perfect harmony. Even his tousled blond hair added to the look of a man who commanded attention everywhere he went.

Aware of her scrutiny, he sent a puzzled glance her way. "What's wrong?"

She laughed. "Nothing. I was just thinking you'd make a good model."

His eyes narrowed. "That's not the kind of life I'd like."

The harsh note in his voice seemed like another reprimand of her previous lifestyle.

Modeling had made her a lot of money, but had also brought her a lot of grief. It had created a false sense of what had value and what didn't. And from the frown on John's face, it had caused an even larger chasm between them.

"It isn't for everyone," she admitted quietly.

"Did you enjoy it? Modeling?"

She easily heard his unspoken questions.

Why did you quit college? Why did you choose Mitch over me?

"I don't think I would have chosen that career if it wasn't for Mitch," Heather responded, trying not to sound defensive.

"He got you your first job, didn't he?"

She gave a curt nod, remembering too well Mitch's promises of big money that had made her quit college when things got hard. And the money had come those first few years. She had been able to repay the Bannisters the sum they had put up for her college expenses, which had made her feel she'd repaid her debt to them. But even as she'd experienced some success, it all came to a crashing halt when Mitch had made some bad investments. The first thing he lost was the fancy apartment, the second, his control over his temper.

Regret, Heather's constant companion, shivered through her.

"I was sorry to hear about your divorce," John said. "I'm sure…it's been hard."

"It's okay. I'm over the worst of it," she told him, with a careful shrug.

Which was a lie, she thought, unable to keep herself from glancing at Adana again. Heather had thought she was over the worst, until she saw John and his perfect little girl—both stark reminders of what she had given up to seek a life she'd thought she'd wanted.

She looked ahead, drawing on old survival skills, tricks she'd learned to get through whatever faced her.

You're on your own, Heather, she reminded herself. *Only you can take care of you.*

"Thanks for bringing our girl home," Monty said, taking one of Heather's suitcases from John as he stepped off the back of his truck. "How badly is Heather's car damaged?"

"Not sure. Dwayne said he would tell Alan to call you and let you know," John said as he set a second suitcase on the ground. "But from what I could see, the front end was badly dented up and the tires had come off the rims."

Monty frowned as he digested that information. "Well, we're glad she's okay."

John nodded, then glanced past him to where Heather stood, hugging her sister. The lights from the ranch house spilled out, casting them in stark relief.

Ellen stood to one side, her arm around Heather's shoulder, her neck brace preventing her from doing more than that.

When the two girls drew apart, Heather kissed her mom carefully on the cheek. Then John saw Ellen gently wipe her adopted daughter's face, her own features looking pained. "Oh, baby girl," he heard her say. "We missed you so much."

"I missed you, too." The broken note in Heather's voice troubled him. She had never been one to share her emotions. To see her so vulnerable created a push-pull of tangled emotions. He shook his head, then turned back to Monty.

"I better get going. Adana is still sleeping, but she's probably hungry. Never did make it to Saddlebank for dinner with Kim and Rex." His in-laws were leaving on a cruise and had hoped to see him and Adana before they left tomorrow. It was too late to go back now.

"Would you like to join us?" Ellen asked.

Heather's head swung toward him the same time he looked her way. It wasn't too hard to see the alarm on her features. Seemed as if she was as anxious about spending time with him as he was with her.

"It's okay," he said, holding up a gloved hand. "I'm sure you have lots to catch up on with Heather. I don't want to impose."

"Oh, since when are you imposing?" Ellen protested. "You eat here plenty."

"And that's why I should let you have some time alone." Sitting with Heather in the truck had been harder than he wanted to admit to himself. She was part of his youth, his past. She'd only ever been his girlfriend, unlike Sandy, who had been his wife.

"Thank you for that," Monty said. He leveled John a steady look, and behind that gaze John sensed an unspoken question.

Was Heather's presence going to cause a problem?

Monty had always been very protective of Heather, a legacy of her troubled past, most likely, and John had always tried to tread carefully where she was concerned. That's why, back in high school, he had waited to date her. That Mitch had beat him to it was poor luck and bad timing. However, when John had finally worked up the nerve to ask her out, it was with fear and trepidation of what Monty would think. Whether he was worthy enough to date the boss's daughter. But once he did, he and Heather had fallen hard for each other. And started making plans.

He had always wondered if the Bannisters had encouraged Heather to go to college precisely to forestall their plans.

Adana's wails from the truck reminded him of his other obligations. His main priority.

"I better get her back to the house," he said, taking a step away.

He caught Monty's nod of approval, and as he walked to the truck John found he had to stifle his frustration. Did Monty still see him only as the foreman's son?

But in spite of his feelings, in spite of their time apart, he couldn't help glancing back at Heather.

Their eyes met and held, John feeling the too-familiar ache in his heart.

He shook it off, turning his attention to Adana. He had his little girl to think of and she needed security and stability in her life.

Heather represented anything but that.

"Got clean tights, diapers, sippy cup, pacifier." John marked off the checklist as he went through the diaper bag. Though his home wasn't that far from the main ranch house, he always liked to make sure Adana had enough provisions for the day.

"Want to go," his daughter said, as he packed up. She scooted away from him toward the back door, as if she knew exactly what was happening next.

"Yeah. I know, munchkin. I'm coming," he said. They were running a little later than usual this morning. After breakfast John had cleaned up the house, did a load of laundry and organized the diaper bag. All in an effort to put off going to the main house.

Monty and Ellen always invited him in for coffee when he brought Adana over, and he always accepted, but Heather was there now.

He hooked the bag over his shoulder, scanning the house to make sure that everything was in order. This was the home he had grown up in, as the son of the foreman. It was compact and simple, and it was home for him and Adana.

It was a cozy place, he reminded himself. Sandy had never wanted to move back to Saddlebank after they got married, preferring their life together in Great Falls. However, there were times he'd imagined the two of them living here, after Monty had offered him a job working on the ranch. But Sandy never wanted to live in their hometown, so the dream had never materialized.

His eyes fell on her photo, sitting by his Bible, both resting on a table by his easy chair. He took a moment to pick up the picture, smiling down at it.

He had taken it a month before Adana was born. Sandy stood in profile to the camera, her hands cupped around the swell of her stomach, her short brown hair teased away from her face by a gentle breeze. Her head was tipped to one side, as if she'd been contemplating the new life growing inside her.

Compared to Heather's sophisticated allure, Sandy looked almost plain, with her freckled complexion and large green eyes. No stunning beauty, she'd always had a beauty of spirit, which had more staying power than Heather's breathtaking looks.

And each moment he'd spent with Sandy, he had grown more and more in love with her.

John touched her picture, sorrow welling up in him at the horrible loss he'd faced when she'd died. Leaving her behind in the hospital while he took his squalling baby home was the hardest thing he'd ever done. He still wasn't sure how he had gotten through the empty months afterward. If it wasn't for his parents, and their invitation to come back and stay with them at Refuge Ranch, he was sure he would have fallen apart. Their support, and Monty and Ellen's help, had brought him through that dark valley to where he was now.

On solid ground with a daughter he loved fiercely. Sandy's little girl.

"I miss you," he whispered to the beloved image in the photo. He waited a moment, as if listening for the giggly laugh that would bubble up every time he tried to get mushy with her.

But the only sound he heard was the happy slap of Adana's hands on the window of the porch door.

He set the picture frame down, straightened it and gave his wife's image a smile. "I told you I would take care of Adana and I will."

He spoke the words aloud, as if to remind himself what was most important right now.

He would need every bit of resolve to get through the unwelcome distraction of Heather at the ranch. It was a good thing she was around for only a week, he thought as he walked toward his daughter, now tugging on the porch door. John could manage if he avoided Heather, which shouldn't be too hard. Cows needed vaccinating before calving. The barn needed to be made ready. Corrals, chutes, gates and fences needed to be checked over and repaired. There was plenty to keep him busy while she was here.

"I go outside," Adana called out, her hands landing on the window again with a carefree splat. She gave John a crooked grin.

"Yes, yes, we're going." He scooped her up in his arms, then held her a moment, looking into her smiling face, her bright blue eyes with their thick lashes, reminding himself that this precious bundle was his main focus.

He gave her a tight hug, holding her close. For a moment she laid her head in the crook of his neck and he inhaled the smell of her—baby shampoo mixed with newly laundered clothes.

"I love you, little girl," he whispered, pressing a kiss to her soft cheek.

Then she giggled and squirmed away from him. Time to go.

He made quick work of getting her jacket and winter hat on. A few minutes later he was dressed as well, and they walked across the yard toward the ranch house, Adana in his arms and her diaper bag slung over his shoulder. The sun was gaining strength, he thought, looking across the yard to the mountains beyond, cradling the basin. He could feel the promise of spring in the warmth on his back and the sound of water trickling across the driveway as the last of the snow melted.

He heard cows bawling, gathered in the lots. They would be calving in a month. If things went well, and Monty accepted his proposal, John would soon be a partner in the ranch. He would have a personal stake in the success and health of the calves.

He wasn't going to jeopardize that in any way.

With that in mind, he headed directly to the main house. Tanner's truck was parked in front. Obviously, Keira's fiancée had come by to see Heather.

John got to the front door and Adana banged her hands on his shoulders, squirming away from him. "No. Not go to house. Go on the wagon," she protested, as he struggled to hold her wriggling body while he opened the door.

As soon as he stepped into the house and tried to set her down, she started crying loudly. The diaper bag slipped off his shoulder and fell to the floor, the contents spilling out.

"Do you need some help?"

John was crouched down, Adana still crying, sitting on his knee as he tried to gather up the cups and diapers, so he had to look up at Heather.

Her hair hung loose today, the morning light from the windows beside the door making it shine. She wore a simple white blouse and blue jeans, and had an empty laundry basket resting on her hip.

She looked so much like the old Heather that his traitorous heart did a slow flip.

He hid his reaction to her by grabbing the diapers, dismayed when he realized that they had been lying in a puddle of melting snow from another pair of cowboy boots.

"Here, let me help you," Heather said, setting the laundry basket on the blanket box and picking up various items that had spilled out. "We'll need to clean these up."

"Pwetty, pwetty," Adana called out, her mood switching with lightning speed.

Except now, instead of reaching for the door, she was leaning toward Heather, arms outstretched. The sudden shift made John wobble on his feet.

"Can you take her?" he asked, trying to not drop everything again as he straightened. Wouldn't that be just amazing, if he ended up on his backside right in front of her.

"Um. Sure." He didn't have time for her hesitation. He shifted his arm, pushing Adana toward Heather. She took the little girl just in time and he managed to regain his balance and keep his pride.

"Guess I can just throw these away," he muttered as he picked up the remaining diapers.

He glanced again at Heather, who held Adana in an awkward grip. He knew Mitch wasn't the kid type. He had made that loud and clear at his bachelor party. But John had always thought Heather would want children.

Her forced smile and the self-conscious way she held his little girl showed him quite clearly how different Heather was from the girl he had once dated.

"I'll take her now," he said, setting the diaper bag back on the floor and reaching for his daughter. "Come on, sweetie."

But Adana ignored him. Instead, she had her hands planted on Heather's shoulders, grinning as she babbled away, clearly fascinated by her. "Pwetty, pretty," she said.

"I think she likes my earrings." Heather seemed uncomfortable, her expression hesitant.

But Adana wasn't looking at the pearls hanging from Heather's ears; her eyes were on Heather's face.

"Probably," John agreed. He caught Adana under the arms and was about to pull her away when she screeched her objection.

"No! No, Daddy! Pwetty!" She leaned away from him, then laid her head on Heather's shoulder.

Heather shot him a flustered look. "I'm sorry."

He didn't know why his daughter had suddenly formed this attachment to a woman she didn't know. Adana was an easygoing girl, but she didn't quickly go to strangers.

Heather turned then, shifting her arms so that John could more easily take Adana from him.

"Hey, you two, are you coming in or are you going to keep yapping?" Tanner called out from the dining room.

Heather gave John an apologetic look, then walked into the kitchen. With Adana wriggling in his arms, he followed her.

"Hey, John." Tanner leaned back in his chair, grinning as Heather sat down. "Coffee's on. May as well join us. Monty's in no rush to head out to feed cows this morning."

John glanced around the room. Tanner, the son of the neighboring landowner, Monty and his two daughters were all sitting around the table.

And there he was, the son of the foreman, standing awkwardly, feeling like the outsider.

"Sure. I'll join you," he said, as Keira got up to take Adana from him.

"Hey, muffin," Keira said, cuddling the little girl close. "You're as cute as ever."

John walked over to the coffeepot, grabbed a mug from the cupboard and poured himself a cup. He knew his way around this kitchen as well as his own.

"So, John, what's Monty got you doing today?" Tanner asked.

"Got some fences to fix," he replied. "The corrals

need a few repairs." He looked to Monty. "You still figure on processing the cows on Saturday?"

"I got that part for the hay bind coming in on Saturday morning first thing, but yeah. After that we can get 'er done."

"I'll have the cows ready to go, then," John said, taking a sip of his coffee.

"You know, I could use a capable guy like you at my place," Tanner said, grinning at him. "Why don't you quit working for this character and come work for me?"

"You trying to poach my best hand?" Monty protested.

"Never hurts to ask," Tanner said with an unapologetic shrug.

"John's a Refuge Ranch man," Monty said, with a broad grin. "Just like his daddy before him."

John tried to tamp down his reaction to the banter between Monty and Tanner. Right now that was his reality. He was only the foreman like his daddy before him.

He thought of the proposal sitting in Monty's office. Now that he was so close, he wanted it done. Then he glanced over at Heather, just as she looked up at him. Their eyes met and she looked away. But even in that brief moment, he was disappointed at how quickly the old feelings taunted him.

He turned to his daughter, feeling a need to get back to work. To keep himself busy. "Hey, muffin, Daddy has to go to work. Wanna sit with me before I go?"

Adana looked at him, then her eyes skittered to

Heather. "Wanna sit her," she said, wriggling away from John's outstretched hands.

"C'mon, honey. Come sit with Daddy," he coaxed.

"Sit her," she insisted. Before anyone could stop her, she slid off Keira's lap, scooted around John's chair and headed straight to Heather.

"Guess you got dumped by your own daughter," Tanner teased.

John was far too aware of the irony of the situation. Getting dumped by his daughter in favor of the woman who had dumped him.

He caught the look of wariness on Heather's face as Adana toddled up to her, then her discomfort as the child tried to climb up on her lap.

John was just about to rescue his daughter when Heather finally picked her up. But Adana wasn't simply content with sitting on her lap. She had another mission in mind.

"Pwetty earrings," she said, reaching for Heather's earrings again, a cluster of chains with a pearl on the end of each. Heather caught her hand and eased it down, the stilted smile on her face making her look as if she would rather be doing anything else than holding his little girl. It bothered him that someone wouldn't want to hold his precious daughter. That it was Heather struck him to the very core.

Suddenly the phone rang, and Keira jumped up from the table to answer it. She spoke for a few moments, then came over to the table, holding it out to Heather. "It's for you. It's Alan, the mechanic."

Heather passed Adana to her sister with a look of relief, then grabbed the phone. "Hello?" She jumped to her feet. "Really? That long?" She bit her lip, then nodded, and finally ended the call.

"So? What's the verdict?" Monty asked.

"Alan said that he had to order some parts and they wouldn't be here for a week to ten days."

"So you'll be around longer?" Keira whooped, obviously more pleased with the news than her sister.

"It looks like it," Heather said, reluctance tingeing her voice.

John knew exactly how she felt. He sighed and then once again caught her looking at him.

Unwanted and unbidden, attraction sparked between them. He tore his gaze away as frustration edged with an older, deeper emotion lay hold of him.

How was he going to avoid Heather for two weeks and still keep his own heart whole?

Chapter Three

Heather sat down, her mind whirling as she tried to think. She had the job interview soon in Seattle, but now had no way of getting there.

She needed that job. Her shrunken bank account was a testament to how quickly she needed to get to work.

But she couldn't get to the interview if she didn't have a car. Her stomach roiled at the thought of the new charges she would have to put on a credit card she had finally cleared off.

Don't look around the corner. Just do what comes next.

The words that had gotten her through the past few years of her life came back to her, but now, in the cozy warmth of her parents' house, they seemed empty. Devoid of the comfort they usually brought her.

"So will you be able to stay until the bridal shower?" Keira asked.

It wasn't too hard to see the sparkle in her eyes and hear the hope in her voice.

"I don't have much choice," Heather said, realizing how reluctant she sounded. She pinned a bright smile on her face, then glanced again at John, who was still watching her. He seemed as thrilled about the idea of her staying the extra time as she was.

"I better get going," he said, setting his mug on the counter. "I'll feed the cows, Monty. You stay and visit."

Then he turned and left.

Heather watched him stride away, his broad shoulders giving him an air of control. He had changed since she'd last seen him, become more reserved. This was not the warm, loving John she remembered.

The distance between them was wider than Judith Basin County. She wasn't sure why it bothered her. She had no intention of taking up where she and John had left off. Both of them had moved far away from that one happy time in her life.

You made your choice when you ignored his advice and went with Mitch to New York.

Past choices melded with present circumstances and she knew that her life was, to some degree, of her own making.

She dragged her attention back to her family, who were all watching her as if waiting to see what she was going to do next.

"I need to make another call," she said. "Can I use the phone in the study?" she asked her father, needing some privacy.

"You go ahead, my dear," he said, waving her on.

"And I should get going," Keira said, getting up,

as well. "I'll be at my workshop," she told Heather. "Come on by and we can make some shower plans."

"Of course," Heather said, thankful that her sister was happy with the situation. She turned to her father. "Are you okay to watch Adana?"

"Alice should be finished soon helping your mother get ready for the day. I think I can manage until then," he said with a grin.

Heather returned his smile, then left. As she closed the door of her father's office behind her, she shut off the sound of conversation that had started up again. She leaned against the door a moment, trying to suppress the panic slowly gaining momentum in her mind.

She couldn't afford a huge repair bill. She couldn't afford to be late for this interview.

She stopped herself. Don't borrow trouble, her father always used to say. So she sat in his large leather chair and with trembling fingers pulled up the information from her cell phone, then made the call.

Very quickly she was put through to Michelle Pearson, the manager she hoped to be working for.

"Good morning, Michelle," Heather said, pulling out her "so happy to see you" attitude and hoping that would generate a positive tone in her voice. In previous conversations they'd chatted about the industry, traded small talk, discussed fashion trends, but right now she just wanted to cut to the heart of the matter. "I'm sorry to tell you that I had an accident. I'm fine but my car isn't. And it won't be fixed in time for me to arrive in Seattle when I said I would."

"Oh. I see." The silence that followed that comment held a heaviness that weighed on Heather. "That changes things. We needed someone quite soon. And we interviewed our second prospect yesterday. My partner was very excited about her, so if you can't come for a week, we may hire her instead."

Disappointment sat like a rock in Heather's stomach. She wanted to protest that they should at least give her a try, but how could she when she couldn't make the scheduled interview?

"We will, of course, reimburse your travel expenses," Michelle added. "Just send me the details of your mileage and associated costs and we can cover those for you."

That was a help, but not much. "Thanks. I'll do that," Heather managed to choke out, feeling the usual burst of shame at the thought that she would probably follow through on collecting even that small amount of money. "And thank you for the opportunity."

"If anything comes up that we think you would be suited for, we'll give you a call," Michelle said brightly, but Heather suspected her promise was more polite than actual. "As a former model, you have a view on the industry that I'm sure we could utilize sometime."

Former model. All part of a very ragged résumé.

Former barrel racer. Former college student. Former wife.

Heather said a polite goodbye, hung up the phone and leaned back in her father's chair, turning it to face the window, giving herself a moment to pull together the tatters of her life. From here she could look out over the summer pasture and then to the hills beyond, rolling up to the mountains that edged the basin. She had ridden those hills with Keira, Lee and John, and knew most every knoll, valley and crevice. The life she'd lived here was like a wash of light in the darkness of her years with an abusive natural mother and her time with Mitch.

Help me, Lord.

The prayer spilled out of her as she swung back and forth in the chair. Then she caught her sad reflection in the office window. She lifted her chin and pushed herself erect. Though she wasn't born one, she'd been raised a Bannister. Life didn't push a Bannister down.

As she stood, she caught sight of John walking across the yard. Once again she felt the regrets of the past slip into the present.

If only she hadn't gone away to school. If only she'd listened to him. If only she hadn't broken up with him. If only she had told him the truth about why she'd wanted to work for Mitch.

As if he sensed her thoughts, John looked back over his shoulder at the house. Heather lifted her hand to touch the window as if to make a connection with him.

Then he seemed to shake his head, shove his hands in his pockets and keep walking.

Heather squared her own shoulders and turned away from the window. She had other things to deal with.

When she came back to the dining room, she walked over to where her mother sat.

"How are you feeling?" Heather asked her as she bent over to give her a kiss.

"Much better. I slept well."

"I'm so glad." Heather glanced over at Alice. "And good morning to you, Alice," she said to the older woman, sitting with a cup of coffee in front of her, feeding Adana bits of her muffin. "Good to see you again."

"Welcome home. I was sorry to hear about your car, but glad that you're okay."

"Thank you," was all Heather said. She liked Alice well enough, but had never felt entirely comfortable around her. Alice had told her often how lucky she was to be taken in by the Bannisters, and had subtly reminded her of the debt she owed this family.

"Were you able to reschedule the interview?" her mother asked with an optimism Heather wished she could channel.

"No. They decided to hire someone else."

"Oh, honey. I'm so sorry." The disappointment in her voice only seemed to add to Heather's sense of failure.

"There'll be other work," she said, pasting on the same smile that she used when she was working the cameras, trying to look excited to be wearing a bathing suit while a chilly wind blew.

"I understand from your mother that you'll be around the ranch for a few weeks," Alice said, cradling her cup of coffee in her hands, lifting one eyebrow as if in query.

"I'm here until my car is fixed," Heather said, going to pour herself another cup of coffee. And while she was here, she would be sending out her résumé to whoever she could.

"That could work out well for me," Alice continued. "I just got a call from my aunt this morning. She's not been feeling well. If you're going to be here, I could visit her. Your mother is still fragile and I wouldn't feel right leaving her and Adana alone. Keira is busy with her work and wedding plans, so I don't think it would be fair to ask her."

Heather sneaked a quick glance toward Adana, who was noisily sucking back a sippy cup of milk. She put her cup down and grinned, showing her tiny top teeth. "Hi, Hevver," she said.

Heather's heart warmed at the sound of the little girl saying her name. Obviously she was as smart as her mother.

"If it doesn't work, I can reschedule…" As Alice's sentence trailed off, Heather guessed the woman sensed her hesitation.

"Or we could find somebody else," Ellen said.

Heather caught her mother's rueful smile and hastily put her hand on her arm, hoping and praying that her mom didn't think her lack of enthusiasm had anything to do with her.

"Of course I can help out today," Heather quickly said, giving her a reassuring look. She was free for the next few days. The least she could do was help where she was needed.

"That's wonderful," Alice said, sounding relieved. "Would you mind terribly if I left right away?"

So soon?

"Sure. That'd be fine," Heather said with a confidence she certainly didn't feel. "Just tell me what I need to do for my mother, and I'm sure I can figure out what to do with Adana. How hard can it be to take care of a toddler?"

"Not hard at all. She's a little sweetheart," Ellen said, reaching over and tucking Adana's bib under her chin.

The child banged her cup on her tray table, then looked at the gathered women, as if sensing the conversation was about her. She gurgled in pleasure at the attention, happily oblivious to the gnawing pain in Heather's soul that her very presence created.

It's just for today, Heather told herself. She could handle it for one day.

"You're good to go," John called out to Monty as he pushed on the fence tightener.

Down the fence line, he could see the rancher swinging his hammer, pounding in the staples on the barbed wire that John had just pulled taut.

They had been busy all afternoon, wading through mud, the occasional snowdrift and sometimes walking on bare ground, working their way down the fence toward the home place, getting the calving area ready. In a month they would be busy, calving out cows. The sun beating down on John's back was a promise of the warmer weather coming.

Soon, he thought, pounding the last nail on his end and pulling off the tightener. He glanced up at the hills, which were already bare of snow, and across the pasture, where only a few drifts leftover from the last storm lay stranded against fence and tree lines.

He dropped the hammer in his pail of tools and

lifted it off the ground. In only a few days, the drifts had receded substantially, leaving mud in their wake.

On Saturday they had to process the cows and give them their precalving shots. He wasn't looking forward to herding them through all this dirt.

"So, we done with this?" Monty called out as he strode toward him.

"That was the last of it," John said.

"Good. I'll head over to the corrals and check them once more before we have to run all the cows through." He nodded toward the house. "You just take a moment to say hi to your little girl."

A high-pitched squeal of laughter caught John's attention and his smile grew.

But when he turned, he frowned at what he saw. Heather was pulling a high-sided wagon. Adana sat inside, leaning over the edge, staring at the ground rolling past her as if it was the most interesting thing in the world.

His eyes reluctantly touched on Heather, who was looking everywhere but at him. She had put a down vest over her shirt, a concession to the brisk spring weather.

Though she still looked as if she was heading to a fashion shoot, the down-home clothes were a reminder of happier times. When they would go out riding. When he would watch her run barrels, timing her and coaching her.

He shook his head, as if to dislodge the errant memories he wouldn't allow himself to indulge in.

"Where's Alice?" he asked. He set the pail down and halfheartedly walked toward them. They met halfway between the pens and the house, the tapping of Monty's hammer echoing over the yard.

"Daddy, ride," Adana called out, reaching for him. He picked her up, settling her against his hip.

"She left this morning to visit her aunt," Heather said. "She asked me to help out with Adana while she was gone."

John narrowed his eyes at the thought of Heather taking care of his daughter. "Just for today?"

"It's fine. I…I can manage. I'm not familiar with kids, mind you…"

"I sensed that," he stated, holding Adana a little closer. She laid her head against him, as she often did when she was tired or upset. Did she also feel Heather's discomfort?

He felt the same overwhelming need to protect his daughter that he had felt when he'd brought her home from the hospital. He had made a promise to himself that he would protect her, take care of her and make up for all she had lost.

"That's why I think I should take care of her," he added.

"But you're busy. I thought…I understood that's why Alice and Mom look after her. So you can work?"

"I'll figure a way around it." He glanced down the fence line toward Monty.

Heather lifted her head, staring him down. "You don't think I'm capable."

In spite of the confrontational tone of her voice, he caught a glimpse of hurt in her features. His resolve wavered a moment, but then he felt the warmth of Adana's head against his neck.

"It's not how capable you are. It's how willing you are." He sighed for a moment, then continued. "Like I said, I sensed that you're not comfortable around her. I don't want my daughter to feel like she's unwanted."

Heather couldn't hold his gaze. Her eyes, with those impossibly long lashes, lowered protectively. "I'm sorry," she said, her voice barely above a whisper. "I know how it looks. It's just…she reminds me…" She stopped there, her hands twisting together.

She seemed genuinely upset.

"Reminds you of…" he prodded.

She bit her lip, shook her head, then slowly, almost reluctantly, looked up. He caught the faintest shimmer of tears in her eyes. "Doesn't matter," she said. "Adana is a sweet little girl and I don't mind taking care of her."

But John couldn't ignore the brief glimpse of sorrow in her eyes and in her voice. Older emotions sifted into the moment and he thought of her upbringing. "Is this because of your mother?"

She frowned and he realized he'd barked up the wrong tree.

"No. Nothing to do with her." She waved off his comment with one hand. But that didn't erase his curiosity. There was more to this than she was letting on.

"I can take care of her," Heather said, reaching out for his daughter. "I know you and Dad have a lot of work to do before calving."

Still John hesitated, glancing from Heather to Monty. He had to be realistic. He couldn't take care of his daughter today.

Then Adana made up his mind for him. She patted him on the cheek with one chubby hand, as if to reassure him, then stretched her arms out toward Heather, her fingers clenching and unclenching.

"Pwease. Go for wide."

John shifted to accommodate Adana's sudden movement, then reluctantly let Heather take her out of his arms. Somehow, in spite of the woman's hesitation around his daughter, Adana seemed to connect with her.

Heather held her for a moment, looking down at her. The tiny quiver of her lips was the faintest tell, raising a host of other questions. There was more to this than mere discomfort around children. There was real pain in her eyes.

But as Monty called out to him again, John knew this wasn't the time or place to find out.

Besides, he didn't have the right to pry into her personal life, he reminded himself as he watched her gently place Adana back in the wagon. He had to keep her at a distance. He had plans for his life, and she would only complicate them.

She gave him a forced smile that he sensed was more for show than anything, then picked up the wagon handle and walked past him.

He didn't plan to watch her leave, but couldn't keep his eyes from following her slim form, her blond hair flowing down her back, glistening in the sun as she headed toward Keira's workshop.

Monty walked over to find out what the delay was. "Everything okay?" he asked John, glancing from him to Heather.

"Yeah. Heather is taking care of Adana. She just brought her by to say hi."

John saw Monty watching him, his eyes intent.

They were both quiet a moment, as if measuring each other.

"Heather hasn't told us much about her life in New York, but her mother and I sense she's had a tough go the past few years," the older man said quietly, folding his arms over his chest, his eyes slipping back to Heather. "Mitch wasn't good for her. She's a very wounded soul."

John sensed a warning in Monty's voice, and wanted to remind him that he had tried to tell Heather not to go with Mitch to New York. Not to believe the promises he had made her.

But he kept his comments to himself, aware of how precarious his current situation was. Even though Heather had been the one to break up with him, his love for her had never been a secret on the Bannister ranch. When Mitch had come to Saddlebank the first time and swept Heather off her feet, Monty had been the one to commiserate with John.

Now, it seemed, he was obliquely warning him to keep his distance.

"If that's the case, Heather will need this time with your family to recuperate before she moves on," John said. "And I wish her only the best in everything she does." He met and held Monty's gaze. "As for me, I have Adana to take care of right now."

The rancher smiled carefully and nodded. "Of course you do." He shifted his hammer from one hand to the other. "I guess we should get this fence fixed before the day slips away from us."

He walked away. But in spite of Monty's warnings, John couldn't prevent another glance over his shoulder to where Heather had stopped and was lifting Adana out of the wagon.

Their eyes met across the yard and once again John felt as if time had wheeled backward. His foolish heart gave a thump.

He had to focus on Adana.

His and Sandy's daughter, he reminded himself. A woman who was faithful and true.

And uncomplicated.

Chapter Four

Adana toddled around the saddle workshop, jingling the bell that Keira had given her. Sugar, the farm dog, followed her around the room as if guarding her.

"She's such a cutie patootie," Keira said, laughing as Adana stopped to tug on the stirrup of a saddle that Keira had been working on.

"She is," Heather said, letting the melancholy note she struggled so hard to keep at bay slip into her voice as she leaned against the workbench.

Her sister had been cutting some leather for a saddle when she and Adana came into the shop, but had gladly taken a break.

Keira shot her a sharp look. "Are you okay? You seem upset."

Heather tried to brush off her concern. "It's just hard…coming back."

Keira boosted herself up on the bench, as if settling in for a chat. "Coming back to the ranch or coming back to John?"

"That was a long time ago," she said, trying to

sound more casual than she felt. "Besides, we've both moved on. He has Adana and I have a new career I'm trying to get established."

"But he's a widower and you're divorced."

"Not going down that road again," she said with a degree of finality.

Adana giggled and shook her bell again. Heather felt her heart compress at the sound.

"There's something else happening," Keira pressed. "You seem so sad. You look tired and seem as if you've lost weight."

Heather gave her sister a reassuring grin. "That's music to any model's ears."

But Keira didn't smile at her feeble joke, just wrapped her arm around Heather's shoulders. "We've got lots to catch up on, you know."

"I know we do," she agreed, slipping her own arm around Keira's waist and returning her hug. "I'm glad to be around you again."

Adana giggled, and Heather sighed lightly.

"There's something else going on. Tell me," Keira said.

Heather didn't want to go back there, to that place, but she also knew her sister wouldn't quit until she told her.

"It's just that Adana is the same age as my…" Heather's voice quavered, but she was determined not to break down. "Sorry. I don't know why I'm so weepy."

Keira's features crumpled as she tightened her arm. "Oh, honey. I never thought…never even put it together."

"It's okay." Heather cut her off, surprised at the way her throat seemed to close up. "It was two years ago. And it wasn't as if the baby was full-term." But she pressed her lips together again, blaming the weariness that had clung to her all morning for her wavering feelings.

She hadn't slept much last night, her thoughts a tangle of old emotions, memories and new difficulties. She had left New York determined to start over. To be independent.

But it seemed that in the space of twelve hours her new start had been easily derailed. Now she had no job, no car and no real prospects on the horizon. Her life was the same jumbled mess as when she'd been living with her biological mother, then with Mitch.

And now seeing Adana, she was faced with the reminder of two of the biggest losses in her life: her baby and John.

"You were far enough along that Mom was buying wool to knit baby sweaters." Keira squeezed Heather's shoulders. "I wish you would have come home after you lost the baby. I know Mom had a hard time with it all. I mean, first grandchild and all, so I can't imagine how hard it must have been for you, stuck by yourself in that apartment in New York."

Heather sucked in a long, deep breath, wishing she could erase the sadness that clawed at her. "It was hard. But you know, if I'd had the baby, it would have meant I would always be connected to Mitch."

"I thought you said he never really wanted kids."

"He didn't, but he's manipulative enough that he would have exercised every right he felt was his."

"Mitch was a jerk. Actually, he probably still is," Keira proclaimed. "I know it's hard for you to be divorced. I'm still glad you two are done."

Heather nodded, recognizing the truth in those words, but unable to repress the ever-present shame that came with the choices she had made.

"Have you talked to Mitch at all since…"

"Since the divorce?" She shook her head. "No. Once everything was over, I told him that I didn't want to have anything more to do with him. It's been a relief not seeing him."

That was so true, in spite of the other actuality of the divorce. The fact that Mitch had cleaned out the bank account she had so painstakingly built up. The thought could still send shame blasting through her, hot, destructive and pointless.

It also had her sitting at the computer checking out other jobs online, sending her résumé to whoever would accept electronic submissions.

"Well, he was a louse," Keira said, her eyes narrowing. "And there's no humiliation in being divorced from someone like him."

Her shame had deeper facets, Heather thought, but she just stepped back and gave her sister a tight smile. "I've missed you so much," she admitted, holding Keira's soft green eyes.

"I missed you, too," Keira returned.

"I'm sorry I wasn't the best sister to you," Heather added soberly. "You've had your own sorrows and struggles."

Keira's gentle look acknowledged the sympathy. "It was hard, but I have Tanner and he's been my rock.

God has also been my refuge and strength. I feel as if I've been surrounded and supported."

Heather felt a twinge of jealousy. "I'm glad for you. I wish I could share your faith in God."

"He's always there," Keira said quietly. "He hasn't moved."

Heather wasn't so sure about that, but wasn't going to get into a theological discussion about God with her sister. Especially when she seemed to be able to draw strength from him.

The jingle of Adana's bell caught their attention. The little girl looked over at them with a grin, as if seeking a reaction. Then she fell down on her bottom and let out an indignant cry. Sugar whined, as if pleading with them to fix something he could do nothing about.

"I'll get her," Keira said, walking away from the workbench. Heather sighed as she watched her sister pick up the little girl. Keira seemed so natural with her.

Then Adana reached out to Heather, as she had been doing since their first meeting. The bell she was holding jingled lightly. "You hold me, pwease," she said, her meaning clear.

"I don't know why she's so stuck on me," Heather said, taking her.

Keira shrugged. "Maybe she knows you need to be around her to get over your own sadness."

Heather held Adana, feeling her warmth seep through her vest and shirt, her heart hitching again at having the little girl in her arms. "Like that therapy they do, when you're afraid of something and you're constantly exposed to it until you get used to it?"

Keira smiled. "Sometimes we need to face our fear in order to conquer it."

Heather guessed she was referring to the shadows in her own life. The shame of being assaulted by Tanner's brother years ago, and how she'd kept it to herself for so long.

"You would know," she said quietly.

"I'm guessing there are still things in your life that you don't want to talk about," Keira said, folding her arms over her chest. "And I'm not going to push you on that. The one thing I realized from my own life is that you can't face the past until you feel like you're in a safe place. And you are in a safe place now. You always said that for you, the ranch lived up to its name. That it was a true refuge."

"It was and it is," Heather said. "This is home."

"And how has it been seeing John again?" Keira prompted.

Heather weighed the question, trying to sort out the unwelcome emotions John evoked.

"He's part of the past I don't necessarily need to face, but do want to leave behind," she finally said. "He was married to an amazing woman and has a kid, and that's the end of that. John and I have both moved on."

Heather wished she could have delivered her speech with more conviction, but her reaction to John belied any protestation she could make.

The skeptical look on her sister's face showed Heather she needed to work on that. Because there was no way she was going to allow herself to be so vulnerable again.

She had spent too much time there and it wasn't happening anymore.

Don't brush your hair. Just wash up and go into the dining room.

John cast a critical glance at his reflection in the mirror as he dried his hands on the towel on the bathroom counter at the Bannisters' ranch house. His hair was dented from his cowboy hat and it stuck up in the back.

Heather would just have to take him as he was, he thought as he hung the towel up and walked out of the bathroom.

As he went past the porch and into the kitchen, he wished he had insisted that he and Adana have lunch in their own house, as he had the past couple days.

Yesterday he and Monty had been busy until suppertime fixing fences, getting ready for today. But he'd picked up Adana and taken her to the Grill and Chill in town, using a need to visit Gord, the owner, as a reason for not joining the Bannisters when he was invited.

This morning he'd brought Adana over right after breakfast and made sure that he'd scooted out of there fast, using the cows as the perfect excuse. But he didn't have to rush. Monty had gone to Great Falls for the part for the hay bind. He had told John to wait on moving the cows until he came back, but John needed to keep busy and out of the house, so he'd gotten them all gathered in the sorting pens. But he couldn't keep avoiding the family, so this morning he had accepted the standing invitation to join them for lunch.

Heather stood by the large table and was ladling soup into bowls as he came into the dining room. She glanced up when he walked in, then quickly looked away, underlining the awkwardness that surrounded any encounter they had. She wore blue jeans again, but her silk shirt negated the down-home effect.

He bent over and kissed Adana's forehead. "Hey, sweetie," he said, brushing his hand over her curls and smiling down at her. "You have a good morning?"

"Hi, Daddy." She grinned up at him, then looked back at the bowl Alice set in front of her. "Yummy soup," she said, picking up her spoon.

"How's your aunt?" John asked Alice, his eyes shifting against his will back to Heather.

"She's not doing as well as I hoped. I think I'll spend a few more days with her," the woman said, breaking some crackers into Adana's soup. "She's still fairly fragile, and now that Heather is staying longer, I'm hoping she can help take care of Ellen and Adana so I can go."

John felt a moment's anxiety. Heather taking care of his daughter more than just for an afternoon? He glanced her way and met her eyes. Once again he sensed her hesitation, then she blinked and the moment was gone.

Maybe he could find someone else to take care of Adana till Alice returned. He couldn't ask his in-laws. They were gone. But there had to be someone who was willing to come out to Refuge Ranch.

"How's Adana been?" John inquired, turning his attention back to his daughter.

"She's been a little angel," Alice said. "But she's getting tired."

"Where's Keira?" he asked next as he picked up the small spoon Adana always used.

"Keira and Tanner went into Bozeman to talk to the wedding photographer," Ellen said, stifling a yawn. "And Monty called. He's still waiting in Great Falls for that tractor part that was supposed to come in on special order today. He didn't think it was worth his while to drive back when the delivery is supposed to arrive at any moment." She gave him an apologetic look. "Hope that's not a problem."

John tried not to sigh. "I've got the herd locked up. I was going to give them their precalving shots. Monty was going to cut the cows for me and run them through."

"And neither Alice nor I can help you," Ellen said.

"I can't wait until Monty comes back to process them." There was no way John could sort and run the entire herd through this afternoon on his own. "I'll have to let them out."

He gave Adana another spoonful of soup and, in spite of his frustration, smiled as she caught his wrist, bringing the spoon closer to her mouth.

"That's a nuisance," Ellen said. "I'm sorry Monty didn't think this all the way through."

"It's okay. We'll just have to try again Monday."

"But cows are always harder to get in the second time, aren't they?" Heather asked.

Her quiet comment drew John's attention to her. He was surprised she knew that.

"And Monty is taking me to Helena to see the specialist on Monday, then we're joining Tanner and Keira at the cattle show in Missoula," Ellen added.

John gave a quick nod as his plans grew more tangled. Monty, she, Keira and Tanner had planned to attend the cattle show, and he had encouraged them to go. He had figured on Alice helping him with Adana. If they'd gotten the cows processed today, he could easily take care of everything else on his own until everyone else came back.

"Plus it's supposed to rain tomorrow," Heather interjected. "That will make it a lot worse to do on Monday, won't it?"

"That it will," he said with a quick sigh.

"So let me help."

Her simple statement caught him off guard. "What?"

"I can help. I've done it before. If you've got the cows all gathered up, it's not that difficult. I can saddle up and cut them out."

"It's hard, dirty work," Alice said. "Are you sure you're up to it?"

"You don't need to do this," Ellen stated, her voice quiet and placating. "You never liked helping with the cows before."

Heather looked from Ellen to Alice to John. "I've helped with the cows before."

And you sulked the entire time, John wanted to add, remembering how she would flounce through her jobs as if she wanted to be anywhere else but helping with those "stinky old cows" as she used to call them. But on the Bannister ranch, when work needed to be done, everyone was expected to pitch in, and when the job was big enough, even Princess Heather had to help out.

"I can help load syringes and move cows," she said. "I know what needs to be done and how to do it."

Still John hesitated, unable to stop from eyeing her current clothes, which were totally unsuitable for the hard, dirty work. She shoved the sleeves of her silk shirt up her arms, as if already preparing herself for the job. "Just let me help," she insisted. "Please."

It was the *please* that finally convinced him.

"Okay. I won't say no," he said, still surprised at her offer. "But don't say I didn't warn you, Princess."

Her eyes narrowed at the reference to her childhood nickname. The one her brother, Lee, had used liberally whenever she'd shirked her chores.

"You don't need to warn me. I know what needs to be done," she said with some force.

John guessed her defensiveness had as much to do with his use of her nickname as his doubt that she could help.

He'd always liked to tease Heather about keeping him on his toes. How she could be so different at times.

It seemed that over the years she had retained that ability. He still wasn't sure what to make of her, or why he should care.

Chapter Five

The rain that had been forecast for tomorrow was introducing itself with a light drizzle that was already dripping off the roof, turning the leftover snow into slushy puddles.

Heather pulled her hat—correction, Keira's hat—lower over her forehead and hunched her shoulders against the sudden chill of the cooling air. Sugar was right on her heels as she walked out of the house.

Their dog lived for this kind of work, Heather thought, taking a moment to pat the animal on the head.

Heather herself? Not so much. As she followed John down the path, slipping on the mud the moisture had created, she had a few second thoughts about what she had done.

But Alice's comment, combined with John using her old nickname, had stiffened her resolve. Given her something to prove.

"You sure you want to do this?" he asked as she caught up to him. He glanced at her soft leather designer boots, which were the only ones she owned with the right heel for riding. "I didn't think you'd want to get those dirty."

"They're all I brought, and Keira's feet are smaller than mine. I think Mom threw my old boots out. I don't care about these."

"Since when? You never even liked to get your pants dirty when you were helping," he said.

"At least dirt washes off."

When John shot her a questioning look, Heather wished she had kept the cryptic comment to herself. She could guess what he was thinking. She always liked to look good. Her clothes were important to her.

The past few years, however, she'd changed her priorities. Clothes didn't matter as much, because she knew better what was really important.

"I've got the cows gathered in four pens," John said, as they got closer to the corrals, the noise of the bawling cows increasing with each step. "We've got to get your horse saddled up first. You still remember how?"

Heather tried not to bristle at his question. It bothered her that he thought she had strayed that far from where she'd come.

"Like riding a bike," she said, with an airy wave of her hand.

"I'll get the needles and vaccine ready. You get Rowdy."

She gave him a quick nod, then left for the tack shed, Sugar trotting alongside her.

The building was just around the corner, between the corrals and the barn. As she rolled open the heavy door and stepped inside the large shed, the achingly familiar smells of leather and oil and the pervasive scent of horse washed over her. Nostalgia and yearning followed as she clicked on the light.

Halters and bridles, neatly coiled, hung from hooks along one wall. On the other, saddles of various sizes rested on their racks.

How often had she come running in here, quickly grabbed a halter, then headed out to get her horse? It didn't matter how many hours she had been riding the day before, how many figure-eight patterns she had gone through, how sore she was. Every time she stepped in here, anticipation washed over her.

She pulled a halter off a hook, then found the bridle and saddle Monty had had custom made for her. She ran her hands over the stamping on the cantle, almost worn from years of riding. How many competitions had she ridden in with this saddle under her?

She'd never won very many, but had loved participating. Flying around the arena on Rowdy, reins threaded through her hands, leaning into turns, had made Heather feel fully alive. Barrel racing was the one thing in her life that had given her purpose.

She slung the halter over her shoulder, hooked the bridle on the horn, heaved the saddle and the blanket underneath it off the rack and carried everything outside.

"You stay, Sugar," she said to the dog as she set the saddle on the hitching rail by the horse pasture. Heather climbed over the fence, whistling at the herd of horses standing on a rise a few hundred feet away.

They lifted their heads, then came trotting toward her, Rowdy in front.

Their hooves pounded on the ground as they picked up speed, dirt kicking up behind them. Just before they reached Heather, they slowed, spinning around as Tia, the lead mare, bared her teeth in warning, keeping the other horses in their place.

"Don't be so bossy," Heather declared, holding her hand up. Tia shook her head, as if trying to assert her supremacy, but Heather just kept her palm up in warning and walked past her to where Rowdy stood.

"Can't believe you big, tough guys let that little mare push you around," she said as she reached her mount. He swung his head away at first, but then, as she talked to him, came closer. Heather stroked his neck, rubbed his forelock, then slipped the halter rope around his neck. "Good boy," she whispered, rubbing him again. "Thanks for not making me chase you down."

She knew it was simple pride, but she wanted to show John that she was capable. That in spite of the fancy clothes he'd seen her in, in spite of her modeling career, she was still a cowgirl at heart. Still the girl he had once cared for.

"Not that I want him back," she said to Rowdy as she tied him to the hitching post, voicing her thoughts to the horse. "But I wouldn't mind some simple respect."

Something she'd always sought, she realized as she slid the bit into Rowdy's mouth and buckled the headstall. That was why she had gone to college. So she could show John she was worthy of him. She shook off the memories, relegating them to the past. She shouldn't want or need John's respect anymore. She was her own person now.

She pulled the saddle off the rail, set it aside, then laid the blanket high on Rowdy's withers and slid it back a bit, just as Monty had taught her.

A few minutes later, she had the cinch tied up snug, the running martingale secured. She took a moment to tug on the stirrups and then walk around Rowdy. It had been years since she'd gotten up on him, and wanted to make sure they understood each other before she climbed on. But as she put her foot in the stirrup, rising up to let him feel her weight, Rowdy stood perfectly still, the only movement from him a twitch of his tail and a flick of one ear.

"Thanks, buddy," she said, patting him on his shoulder as she settled in the saddle, shifting her weight to make sure the stirrups were still the right length. But all was well. "Let's go work some cows," she told him.

As she set out, she felt the rise of anticipation from being atop a horse. In spite of the drizzle, a sense of well-being rushed over her. She had a feeling of rightness. Of being exactly where she should be.

John was already on the walkway as she came near, standing slightly above her.

"We're ready," she said.

"That didn't take long."

"He was right there. I think he was happy to see me, weren't you, boy?" she said, rubbing her hand over Rowdy's mane. "We're going to have to go for a ride when this weather eases up." Heather squinted up at the low-hanging clouds, unable to keep from smiling as she thought about going out into the hills.

"Not the best day to work cows," he said, squinting up at the leaden clouds in turn.

"But Monday will be worse. So let's just get it done."

"Okay. Here's how we'll do it. I want you to let five cows into the chutes at a time, then close the gate behind them." He shot her a questioning look and she nodded, tucking Rowdy's reins under her arm and tugging on her gloves.

"Only five," he emphasized. "More than that and there's not enough room in the chute for them."

"I think I can count that high." She couldn't stop the slightly sarcastic quip from coming out. "And if I can't, Rowdy can."

John leveled her a wry look. "If you prefer, you can give the shots and I can move the cows around."

Heather shook her head. "I'm better at the counting and sorting. I was never very good at needling. Too scared to jab them hard enough."

"Like that time Lee tried to get you to needle that cow?" John asked with a mocking grin. "I thought you were going to cry."

"I did. Mostly out of frustration because you and Lee kept laughing at me."

"Cows have tough hides," John assured her.

"So you said, but I kept thinking they were going to hate me for hurting them."

John's sardonic grin eased into a smile. "You always were a bit of a softy," he said quietly, his words surprising her.

She looked up at him, his blue eyes holding hers a second longer than necessary.

Her heart slowed at the connection, and for a moment she couldn't look away. It was as if time sped backward and they were just two young kids, eager to spend some time together. Alone.

She shook off her silly reaction. "So, let's get going," she said, bringing herself back into the moment.

She rode over to the corrals, going around the long way. She dismounted and the cows ran away from her, leaving lots of room for her to close the metal gate behind her and Rowdy. When it screeched, they all started bawling again. As she mounted again, she looked over the gathered animals, which were pushing against each other, lifting their heads to moo in protest.

Heather remembered other times that she, Keira, Lee, John and sometimes Tanner would help Monty out with moving the herd. They'd always made a fun day of it in spite of her reluctance. Afterward, they'd have a wiener roast at the same pit that had been there since forever.

Good times.

"Counting the cows?" John called out from his spot above the melee.

"Trying to see if they're divisible by five," she yelled back.

John laughed. "I'm sorry. I shouldn't have sounded so patronizing. I'm just a little uptight about this."

His apology, combined with his genuine smile, melted her resistance. "Of course you are. Dad was supposed to be helping. Instead you're stuck with Princess Heather."

"I'd say that's better than nothing," he said. "But that would be even more patronizing than my counting comment."

Across the space between them, she felt his look, as tangible as a touch. The cows in the pens, the horse under her, all dragged out memories.

Then she turned away from him, nudged Rowdy in the ribs and moved slowly toward the herd. She had a job to do and she was going to do it. She had no right to entertain any thoughts of John. No right to allow any of the old attraction to seep in.

She'd had her chance with him, and she'd messed that up.

The drizzle worked its way down her neck, but she ignored it. Taking in a deep breath, she nudged Rowdy, whistled to Sugar and moved slowly toward the cows, unbunching them. Rowdy cut out five, and with Sugar herding them in the right direction, they got them through the gate that John held open.

She grinned as exactly five went in. Slamming the gate behind them, she gave him a cheeky thumbs-up.

He returned the gesture and Heather felt the tension in her chest ease.

It would be okay. She could do this.

John slammed the gate of the chute behind the next five cows that Heather and Rowdy had sent toward him, then made quick work of giving each animal a shot, though he shivered in the rain that had started up.

Part of him wanted to quit as water ran off his hat and down his neck, but he quelled that. This job had to be finished today.

As soon as he was done, he walked over to the head gate, taking his time on the slippery walkway. "You can send in five more," he yelled over the noise of the cows and the clanging of the gate. The animals in the chute pushed at each other, making the boards creak as they spied freedom beyond.

John glanced back over his shoulder to see if Heather had heard him, but she was already working her horse through the remaining cows, cutting a few away from the herd. Sugar went with her, helping her move them toward the open gate.

She was making her way slowly through the bunch, looking confident and in charge. Her coat held smudges of dirt, her hair hung down her back and the rain had made her mascara run in spite of her cowboy hat.

But it was the smile on her face that caught his attention. In spite of the lousy weather and the chill that was slowly permeating every layer of clothing, she wore an ear-to-ear grin. A genuine smile that looked nothing like the one he saw in the magazines Ellen had saved with Heather's picture on the front.

This expression was the same one she'd had just before every rodeo competition as she'd waited in the alley of the arena, mounted on Rowdy, every muscle in both rider and horse trembling. And when she'd gotten the signal, she would kick Rowdy and bend over him, her face lit up with anticipation.

John watched her for a moment, then caught himself. *Too much living in the past*, he thought as he walked over to the gate to let the cows into the chute. He pushed it open and glanced back at Heather to make sure she was managing all right.

She was leaning sideways, trying to unlatch the gate for the next bunch she and Rowdy had sorted. Though she had done so a number of times, this time she couldn't manage it. Maybe the rain made the latch stick. John was about to go over to help her when she moved Rowdy away from the gate and dismounted.

She tied the reins to the rail, then walked toward the gate. Just as she unlatched it, the cows remaining in the pen suddenly broke toward her, tossing their heads as if in warning.

"Watch out!" John called.

But the animals Heather and Rowdy had cut away caught sight of the ones coming toward them, then turned and spun back just as the others joined them.

In the melee John watched with horror as one of the cows pushed against Heather. Rowdy whinnied as if warning her; Sugar growled, then snapped at the cow's heels, which made it spin around again. Heather grabbed the gate for support, but it swung away and she went down between the cows.

"Heather, Heather," John cried, vaulting over the fence and running down the alleyway. He slipped on the wet wood, but then jumped over the railing into the pen where Heather had fallen.

He couldn't see her.

His heart in his throat, John worked his way along the fence, not wanting to push more cows toward where Heather had fallen, afraid they might spook and trample her.

He heard Sugar yelp, saw a flash of brown and black, a wave of her plumed tail. The cows shook their heads, but moved away. John felt his heart surge with relief when he spotted Heather sitting in the dirt, her pants and coat plastered with mud, her hat askew and one glove missing.

She waved her hands at the cows, yelling at them, and John heard fear in her voice as he climbed over the gate.

The herd had moved a safe distance away by the time he caught her by the arm and hauled her to her feet.

"My glove…" she said, her voice faltering.

"Are you okay?" he asked, scanning her for injuries.

"Yeah. I just slipped in the mud."

John pulled off his own glove, straightened her hat, then gently wiped the mud from her face, his fingers lingering on her cool, weather-damp cheek.

Then he frowned as he saw what the mud had covered up. "You hurt yourself," he said, touching a scrape on her cheek.

It was a small connection, but it sucked the breath out of him.

"It's nothing," she said, pulling back ever so slightly. From the way her hands trembled, he wondered if she was as affected as him. "I…I should get my glove." She sounded as breathless as he felt, and as their eyes met, it seemed as if the very air he was breathing was charged with emotion. As if the very center of his soul had opened up.

The bawling of the cows slowly reminded him of why they were here.

He dragged his gaze away and, looking down, spied her missing glove. He picked it up, then handed it to her, their fingers brushing, a spark of awareness following that simple motion. "Are you sure you're all right?" he asked, trying to cover up his reaction.

"I'm fine. Sorry I didn't deliver your five. I'll get right on it," she said, slipping on her glove.

"We can take a break if you want," he said, still concerned about the mark on her face. "You might want to get that cut cleaned out."

"It's just a scrape. I'll wash up when we're done." She shrugged off his concern, dirt still speckling her cheeks, loose tendrils of damp hair hanging around her face.

He remembered the Heather he used to hang out with. The Heather who used to race madly around barrels he and Lee had set up. The Heather who would help build tree forts and go riding out in the hills.

The Heather he had so easily fallen in love with. He felt a resurgence of the old yearning she could create in him, a crack in the defenses he had spent so long building up against her.

Irritated with himself and his reaction, John spun away. He was supposed to be immune to her. Years ago, Heather had chosen Mitch and a life that had taken her far away from Montana and Refuge Ranch. Far away from him. They were on completely different paths now.

Yet even as his heart kept pounding, he couldn't stop himself from glancing back at her over his shoulder. Heather was pulling her hat farther down on her head and untying Rowdy. In one easy movement she vaulted into the saddle, determined to finish the job.

The girl who hated working with cows, the girl who was always so careful with her clothes, was now slogging through the mud in her designer duds. She confused him and at the same time intrigued him.

With Heather, he knew that was always a dangerous combination.

By late afternoon, they got the last few cows processed. As he opened the head gate to let the last ones leave, he arched his back, working the kinks out. Thankfully, the drizzle had eased off and the clouds were bunching up, allowing glimpses of blue sky through.

"Guess we're all done," Heather called out as she rode Rowdy through the double gates to get to the alleyway where John was standing. Sugar crawled underneath, in a panic to join her.

He grinned at the sight of her—hat askew again, hair damp, mud splatters on her face and vest. And her fancy blue jeans were unrecognizable under a sheen of mud.

"If the designer of those jeans could only see them now, " John called as she rode closer.

Heather grinned, looking down at her filthy pants. "It's good, honest dirt from good, honest work," she returned as she dismounted.

He gathered up the syringes and empty inoculation bottles, dropped them into the plastic container they always used, then jumped off the walkway. "It went good today," he said, giving her an apologetic smile. "Thanks for helping. I'm still a bit surprised."

"To see Princess Heather so dirty?"

"To see her so capable," he replied, tucking the container under his arm. "And not scared of the cows."

"Not so scared when I'm on a horse," she said with a light laugh, looking past him to where a few cows still milled about, as if unsure where they were supposed to go. "Besides, I had something to prove."

"To who?"

"Myself. You." She angled her head to one side as she curled Rowdy's reins around her hand. "I didn't want you thinking I'm incapable of helping."

He eased out a smile. "I'm glad you proved me wrong. It would have been too much work to handle all by myself, and would have taken me three times as long."

Heather stroked Rowdy, then patted Sugar on the head, as if thanking her two companions for their contribution. "So that worked out well. I'm heading up to the house to clean up. Princess Heather can tolerate only so much dirt."

John laughed, then glanced at the scrape on her face, frowning. "How's your cheek?" He resisted the urge to take a closer look.

Heather lifted one gloved hand, as if to check. "It hurts, but it's not a big deal."

"It looks like a medium deal," he said, still concerned.

She laughed. "Keira used to always say that."

John smiled at that. "I know. That's why I said it. But you make sure you clean that up good. I don't want to be the cause of the famous Heather Bannister's disfigurement. I'm sure the designer of your jeans would be more upset about the mark on your face than the dirt on his pants."

Heather released a harsh laugh. "Oh, don't count on it. The model is just something to hang the clothes on. Mitch always said I was easily replaceable."

The hard note in her voice bothered John, as did what she said.

"That wouldn't be the first time that idiot was wrong." As soon as the words left his mouth, he regretted it. "Sorry," he said. "I shouldn't talk about your husband that way."

"*Ex*-husband," Heather corrected as they walked toward the barn, Rowdy plodding along behind her. "Very much ex-husband. And you can call him what you want. I've probably called him worse."

Sadness braided with anger crowded in on John at the bitterness in her voice. He wanted to reach out to touch her. Connect with her. Try to find the old Heather buried in this new, harsh version.

Then she looked up at him, a shadow of the smile she had given Sugar and Rowdy lingering on her lips. "Thanks for letting me help. It was great to be riding again."

He held her eyes a moment, catching yet again a glimpse of the woman he had once cared for so much.

"Make sure to look after that cut," he said quietly.

"Yes, sir," she said, then walked away, her horse following behind her.

As he watched her leave, unable to keep his eyes from her slender form, he felt as if his emotions were a jumbled stew of memories, care and concern.

Then he shook them off. He had work to do. Heather was part of his past. He had to let it go.

Again.

Chapter Six

"Wow, Heather, you look gorgeous."

Heather glanced up from her makeup bag on the bathroom counter and gave her sister, who was standing in the doorway, a self-conscious smile.

"It's not too fancy for church in Saddlebank?" she asked, smoothing one hand down the skirt of the dress she had just finished ironing. The aqua-and-gold-leaf-printed garment was a gift from a designer who had called her in a panic, needing a last-minute runway model. It was a bright contrast to the simple blazer, white shirt and dark pants that Keira wore.

"No. It suits you," her sister said, slipping past Heather and plugging in a curling iron. "You could always pull off clothes that would look too over-the-top on other people."

"So are you saying this is too much? Should I change?"

Keira gave her a puzzled look as she pulled a brush out of one of the drawers. "Where is this coming from? The Heather I knew never cared much what people thought of her."

It came from too many days of listening to Mitch criticizing her, Heather thought. Telling her not to dress like a rodeo princess, and to think like a model instead. Of hearing photographers and makeup people talking about which of her flaws they had to hide, and how to work with what they had.

"I just don't want to look too New York."

"You look really nice," Keira assured her. "And Mom and Dad won't care if you show up in Oscar de la Renta or Target. They're just glad you're coming to church with us."

"Haven't done church for a while," Heather admitted. "I feel like a fraud."

"You know better than that," Keira replied. "You know God is as happy to see you come to church as Mom and Dad are to see you back here at Refuge Ranch."

"I'm glad to be home."

"I know Rowdy sure missed you. What do you say to going for a ride when we come back from the cattle show in Missoula? We won't be home too late and I'll be ready to get out after all that driving."

"Sounds good." Heather smiled at the thought, swiping some blush over her cheeks. Then she leaned forward, checking out the red scrape that stood out on her cheekbone. She'd tried to cover it with foundation, but hadn't been able to hide it completely.

"That looks nasty," Keira said. "Are you sure it's not infected?"

"No. It's just a skin abrasion." She dabbed at it, her

hand slowing as her mind flicked back to that moment when John had touched it and encouraged her to get it bandaged.

His hand on her face had stolen her breath. Had sent an anticipation thrumming through her that was as strong as it was unexpected. One touch and all the years between seemed to have slipped away.

Keira bumped her with her hip. "Hey, you. Coming back to me anytime soon?"

Heather blinked, suddenly self-conscious of her meandering thoughts, realizing that Keira had been asking her a question. "Sorry, what did you say?"

"I was going to ask you how it went yesterday. Needling the cows. You were in bed when I came back from Bozeman."

"I was exhausted," she admitted. "Not used to the physical work and spending so much time outside. But it went good. No major wrecks."

"Other than that scrape on your cheek."

"Minor injury. Good thing I'm not modeling anymore. I'd get into the usual trouble for that."

Keira looked at her reflection, holding her gaze.

"What?" Heather asked, brushing more powder over her scrape.

"I sometimes wonder if you really enjoyed that work," Keira said.

Heather's hands slowed as her thoughts slipped back to that erratic and confusing time of her life. "It was hard always being seen as simply a clothes hanger. I was thankful I wasn't doing haute couture. I wouldn't have survived trying to keep myself so emaciated. Even for the work I did, I was forever watching what I ate, weighing, measuring, never feeling like I was good enough. Mitch didn't help."

"I got the feeling that things weren't good between you two well before you divorced."

Heather tapped the remaining blush off her brush and put it back in her makeup bag. "I should never have married him. It was a mistake."

"Why did you? Marry him?"

She slowly zipped up her bag, then sighed. "I'm not ready to talk about it. Not yet."

"You keep saying that." Keira crossed her arms over her chest. "One of these days you'll have to tell someone. I know there're things you aren't saying that I wish you would trust me with."

Heather toyed with her makeup bag, pulling the zipper tab back and forth, back and forth. "It's not a matter of trusting you," she finally said. "It's a matter of shame."

"Shame about what?"

"Mitch used to beat me."

The words dropped from her lips as if they had a life of their own. As if they had been waiting for this moment to be released. And right behind them came the usual shame. As if she should have done something to stop him.

"What?" Keira's mouth fell open and she stared at her.

"That's why I left him," Heather continued, leeching all emotion out of her voice. This was only the partial truth, but she felt she had given her sister enough for now.

"Oh, honey. You never said…we never knew…"

Keira slipped her arm around Heather's shoulders and pulled her close. "I'm so sorry. Why didn't you tell us?"

"Because I was too ashamed to admit it. Because I kept hoping that his promises to stop were true." She slowly exhaled, a release of some of the tension that had held her since she'd signed the final divorce papers. "I should never have believed him."

"And that's why you divorced him?"

"Partly." She caught the question in Keira's eyes and hastily added, "Mostly. Like I said, I should never have married him. I knew he wasn't a good person."

"Oh, honey. I feel bad that you had to deal with this alone." Keira touched her cheek. "We Bannister women do like to keep things to ourselves, don't we?"

Heather knew her sister was referring to her own secrets. "Well, you didn't have any choice in what happened to you," she said.

"Neither did you."

Heather shook her head. "No. I'm not a victim. I don't want to be seen as a victim."

"Honey, none of us want to be seen that way. I certainly didn't. But the reality is that sometimes life beats us down. We have to find a way to get our feet under us. The way it happened for me was to trust that God loved me as I was, even when I was crushed and lying in the dirt."

Keira's words alighted on Heather's wounded soul and she let them settle, not sure she believed them yet, but also not sure she wanted to dismiss them out of hand.

"I know that on one level," she admitted. "I've

been told it enough. Just hard to feel, sometimes, like I'm worth it."

"You are. In God's eyes, we all are." The conviction in Keira's voice made Heather smile.

"Thanks, honey. You're a treasure."

"So are you. Remember that." Keira shook her finger at her sister and Heather laughed. "In spite of the scratch on your face." Keira touched it again, shaking her head. "I feel bad that I wasn't around to help process the cows, though. And I'm still surprised you were willing to do it."

"Didn't have much choice."

"Of course, it probably didn't hurt that John was around."

Heather couldn't stop the faint blush creeping up her neck. "I just helped because no one else was available," she said, maybe a bit too forcefully.

"Of course you did." Keira gave her a condescending smile and Heather just sighed.

Trouble was, if she were to truly examine her motives for helping, she knew she would find bits of truth in what Keira was saying.

But Heather wasn't going to do that right now. She had to get ready, physically and mentally, for church.

And John was going to be there.

The guitars, drums and voices of the worship team were the first things Heather heard as she stepped into the foyer of the Saddlebank church. The happy and upbeat sounds were a contrast to the usually somber music that Laura McCauley often coaxed out of the old church organ.

"Things have changed," she said to her sister as they hung up their coats. "I didn't think Laura would ever give up her spot as organist."

"She hasn't," Keira said. "But she doesn't play as often."

"So the prodigal daughter has returned home."

Heather glanced over to see Brooke Dillon hurrying toward them, arms open wide. Her old friend grabbed her in a bone-crushing hug, then pulled back, holding Heather by the shoulders as her brown eyes danced up and down her dress. "My goodness, I should have checked before I hugged. That looks expensive. Any designer I know?"

"A young up-and-comer," Heather returned. "I like the hair," she said, fingering Brooke's ombré-toned locks. "Very chic. What does George think?"

"The hair is a work in progress," Brooke said, tucking her arm in Heather's. "And we're not talking about Mr. Bamford at all."

Her angry voice told Heather that the ongoing infatuation Brooke carried for the owner of the Grill and Chill was on the wane.

"So, you'll have to tell me all about New York and your glamorous life," Brooke enthused. "Keira showed me the magazine spread you were featured in. *Très* cool."

Just like old times, she kept up a steady stream of chatter as the three of them made their way into the church.

"I imagine we'll have to save a spot for Tanner and your parents," Brooke said.

"Tanner took his mom to see his aunt in Bozeman," Keira said with a sigh. "And Mom wasn't feeling well this morning so Dad stayed home with her. She wanted to make sure she was rested up for the trip to Helena tomorrow. So it's just us three."

"Awesome. We can go out for coffee afterward."

"To the Grill and Chill?" Heather couldn't help asking, happy to keep the attention off herself.

Brooke just rolled her eyes as the two of them followed Keira up the aisle.

Heather's steps faltered when her sister stepped into a pew, excusing herself as she walked past the lone occupant.

John.

Had she done this deliberately? Heather wondered.

She had no choice but to follow her sister and Brooke. John stood as first Keira, then Brooke walked past him, leaving Heather to sit beside him. Her eyes shifted toward him, only to find him looking at her.

"Your scrape looks better," he said, giving her a cautious smile. "Glad it didn't get infected."

His concern created a surprising warmth. "It's fine. Now I feel more like a country girl."

"You don't look like one," he said. "You look more like a…"

"Like a model," she finished for him, unable to suppress the prickly tone that crept into her voice.

John narrowed his eyes and she immediately felt bad. She didn't need to be so defensive.

Then the pastor came to the front of the church, a handsome young man with thick black hair, unusually bright blue eyes and a warm smile.

"Welcome to the members of Saddlebank Church

and to anyone who might be visiting. We hope and pray this will be a time of fellowship and encouragement."

Heather caught a few people glancing back at her. Some were familiar faces, smiling in welcome, some seemed more curious about why Heather Bannister was back after such a long absence.

She wondered what they saw. Beryl Winson's natural daughter? Monty and Ellen's messed-up, adopted daughter?

Then the music started up again, and as Heather looked toward the front of the church, a fragment of memory returned. It was of the first time she had come to church with the Bannisters, the day after the social worker had dropped her off. Though she'd never been in church before, she'd known enough to dress up, so she'd worn her best skirt and top. Trouble was, the skirt was short and tight. The top was a sequined halter one her mother had bought her. She'd put on the makeup her mom had given her and thought she looked nice.

She still couldn't believe that Ellen had said nothing at all about her clothes. When they got to church, Heather had realized how poorly she had chosen. She'd felt suddenly self-conscious and self-aware.

The next day Ellen had taken her clothes shopping and made some diplomatic suggestions as to what she might want to choose.

Heather had gotten the unspoken message that the clothes she'd owned weren't entirely suitable. She'd never made that mistake again.

The minister asked them to turn to Isaiah 49, and

as he read the passage, Heather followed along in the Bible she had taken from the pew in front of her. Then her heart skipped a beat at the words.

"Can a mother forget the baby at her breast and have no compassion on the child she has borne? Though she may forget, I will not forget you. See, I have engraved you on the palms of my hands; your walls are ever before me."

Pastor Dykstra read on, but Heather returned to the initial passage, her finger tracing the words as they settled into her soul.

The thought of Beryl resurrected an old ache and a forgotten feeling of betrayal. And intertwined with that, the old anger. She was more than thankful that the Bannisters had rescued her from that life, but living with Monty and Ellen and their unconditional love had showed her what she'd missed those first ten years of her life.

She read the words again as Pastor Dykstra began expounding on the passage. She lifted her eyes and heart, and listened.

"…We forget we're a work in progress," Pastor Dykstra said. "Like the Israelites Isaiah was speaking to, we're never done. We turn away from God and return again and again, a spiral of pushing away and being drawn back. We can be frustrated with ourselves and where we are going…or not going. But we need to know that our lives are ever before God. He is building us. Patiently remembering us."

Heather felt the pastor's words flow through her. Her life had been a mess, had fallen apart, but as she listened to Pastor Dykstra, she felt the first rays of hope in a long time.

A feeling that things could come together. That God was watching over her, taking care of her.

A faint prickle teased her neck. Unbidden, her head twisted and she caught John's eye. There was a curious expression on his face, as if he could read her mind.

She gave him a careful smile, and when he returned it, the hope that had made itself known grew. Just a bit.

"Thanks for giving me your cold," John said to Adana as he buttoned up her coat. His ears hurt. "I guess working the cows in the rain Saturday didn't help much."

Yesterday, after church, he would normally have gone to his in-laws for dinner, but they were still away on their cruise. So when they'd come home, while Adana napped, so had he. First time he'd done that in years.

He'd also forgotten to turn on his alarm clock, and was woken up by a text from Monty this morning, saying goodbye. By the time John finally dragged himself out of bed, the Bannisters were gone. He'd taken some cold medication, which was only now slowly starting to kick in.

Somewhat.

"I've got to figure out how to feed the cows and fix the rest of the corrals by myself, feeling like a truck ran over me," he complained as he tossed her diaper bag over his shoulder.

Adana just giggled.

Monty, Ellen, Keira and Tanner weren't supposed to be back until Wednesday afternoon. John just hoped he could get through the next few days on his own. Lousy time to get sick, he thought.

He stepped out of the house and took a moment to enjoy the growing warmth of the sun. "Spring is here, sweetie," he told Adana as he headed toward the Bannister house.

Inside it was eerily quiet. Then, from upstairs, he heard the sound of someone singing slightly off-key, then footsteps hurrying down the stairs.

"Hello," he called out, hanging Adana's diaper bag on a hook on the porch and toeing his boots off. "Anybody home?"

He stepped into the kitchen, still holding his daughter, just as Heather came into the dining room, pail in one hand, mop in the other.

Her hair was pulled back into a ponytail. She wore a blue, filmy shirt tucked into blue jeans and, to his surprise, bare feet.

Her song came to an abrupt halt when she saw him.

"Hey...I was just cleaning...I didn't know when you were coming." Her voice faltered, as if she'd been caught doing something wrong.

"Would you have been singing?" he teased her.

A flush brightened her cheeks, making the mark on her face stand out even more. "Probably not."

John laughed again, which triggered a bout of coughing.

"I may not sound too good, but neither do you,"

she said, setting the pail down and the mop aside. She walked over and took Adana from his arms.

Her spontaneous move surprised him, but he could still see a stiffness when she handled his daughter. A reserve. What was it about Adana that bothered her so?

He coughed again, covering his mouth with his elbow. "Sorry," he said, when he was done. "Just got this cold yesterday."

"How's Adana?"

"She's fine. So you don't have to worry about catching anything from her."

"That's not what I meant," Heather protested, and he quickly realized he had misinterpreted her again. "I just want to make sure she doesn't need any special care."

"Isn't Alice coming?"

Heather shook her head. "Because Mom will be away the next few days, Alice decided to go visit her aunt." She shifted Adana on her hip, glancing from her to John. "I can take care of your daughter, you know."

"I know."

"You don't sound convinced."

"Sorry. I just want to make sure that things will go well." He felt bad that he'd doubted her, but couldn't help remembering her comment about his daughter reminding her of…something? Someone? He wanted to ask, but knew it wasn't his place.

"I'll take good care of her. She'll be easier to deal with than a couple hundred cows." Heather gave him a grin, which in turn made him smile.

"I wouldn't say that too quick," he said. "Cows you can usually convince to get moving, one way or another. If Adana has a notion to do something, she's pretty determined."

"I'm guessing that's more Argall than Panko."

John laughed. "A bit of both." He bent closer and pressed a kiss on Adana's cheek. "Be good for Miss Bannister," he told her, brushing his hand over her head and cupping her cheek. "Daddy will be back for lunch." Then he shot a quick look at Heather. "I mean, I don't have to."

"No. Of course you'll come. Mom and I made soup for lunch and a casserole for supper. If you want to eat supper here, too, that is."

"You always did like to cook," John said. "I remember that time you cooked a full-course meal for the family all by yourself. Appetizers, soup, salad, the works."

"Don't forget dessert."

"How could I? Dad, Mom and I had to come over to help the family finish it off."

"That was a fun day," she said, her smile penetrating the small corner of his heart that he hadn't been completely able to surrender to anyone else. Memories that would always belong to Heather. First dance. First kiss. First love.

Their eyes held a moment longer than necessary.

"It's good to see you around here again," he said.

"It's good to be here," she said, her quiet response surprising him. "And in spite of ruining a very expensive pair of blue jeans, it was good helping you with the cows the other day. I enjoyed doing an honest day's work."

Her smile created an answering warmth in him. "As opposed to a dishonest day's work?" he quipped.

"Like modeling?"

"I wasn't trying to slam what you used to do," he answered, wishing he could be more tactful around Heather. Something about her always made him feel as if he was forever off balance. "I was just trying to make a joke."

"No. I'm sorry. I'm overly defensive about it."

He was quiet for a moment. Then he looked directly at her, suddenly tired of the dancing around they had been doing since they'd met.

"Why is that?" he asked. "That you're defensive about it?"

Heather set a squirming Adana on the floor. The child toddled away, and as Heather's eyes followed, John caught a glimpse of some emotion he couldn't place.

"Before Mitch and I split up," she said, wrapping her arms around her midsection in what seemed like a protective gesture, "I was working for a company I didn't enjoy very much."

Fear clutched his heart. "Doing what?"

"Nothing really bad," she hastened to say, her eyes flying to his. "I mean, nothing explicit. It was just work for a catalog. Bathing suits, swimwear, that kind of thing. It paid well, but…the people I worked for…" She paused, and once again he felt a sense of impending dread.

"Needless to say, they weren't exactly the crème

de la crème of the fashion industry," she continued.
"They treated me and the other girls horribly. Like we
were objects instead of people. I wanted to quit, but
Mitch convinced me to stay. Then, when the catalogs
came out, they made us look way more provocative
than we were. They edited elements into the pictures
that weren't there during the shoot. It wasn't pleasant
to see the end result. That was the last modeling job
I ever did for them. Mitch was furious, but I wasn't
going to be treated that way again."

Her comment about Mitch's anger disturbed John.
It was on the tip of his tongue to ask more, but another fit of coughing seized him, followed by a sudden wave of dizziness. He swayed, reaching out for
the counter.

"Are you okay? You don't look so good." Heather
caught his shoulder, as if to steady him.

Her hand felt warm and he reached up to cover it
with his.

The action was impulsive, and when her eyes wid-
ened, he sensed that it was as surprising to her as it
was to him.

He blinked and shook his head, as if to settle
thoughts that suddenly seemed less clear. This was
Heather, he reminded himself. He couldn't let himself get caught up in her life.

And yet, as one part of his mind told him to leave,
another part revisited older emotions. Once upon a
time, they had been so happy together.

Then the phone rang and the moment was broken.

He gave her a quick nod, looked over at Adana and
blew her a kiss, reminding himself of his priorities.

But as he left the kitchen, left his daughter in the care of his old girlfriend, he couldn't help but glance over his shoulder once more.

Heather wasn't looking at him this time. She was staring down at Adana, an expression of utter sorrow on her face.

He wanted to ask her, yet again, what it was about his daughter that caused this sadness.

But he didn't dare. Doing so would create a connection that would be broken when she left. He didn't think he had the strength to deal with that again.

Chapter Seven

"So, miss, why do you think your father hasn't come to join us?" Heather asked Adana, who was sitting on the floor by the kitchen cupboard, banging on a pot with a wooden spoon. She looked up at Heather and grinned, then returned to her banging. It was already one o'clock and John hadn't come in for lunch yet. Heather and Adana had already eaten, however.

The little girl banged again, as if waiting for a reaction. Heather crouched down to her level and Adana grinned. Once again, Heather had to fight the unwelcome surge of sorrow she felt around the toddler.

"I know it's not your fault, munchkin," she said softly. "But it's hard to be around you."

Adana just smiled at her and Heather felt the walls she'd erected slowly erode. Sorrow scrabbled at her heart, and she took a breath, trying to contain it.

What would her life have been like if she'd carried her baby to term?

With that question came another surge of anger at Mitch.

She pushed the memories down, but it was like

trying to put spilled water back in a cup. Along with the images came the emotions that had overwhelmed her after she and Mitch had separated.

Please help me, Lord, she prayed as she fought for control. *You said that my walls are ever before You. Help me to keep those walls sturdy and solid. Help me not let Mitch take over my life again and break them down.*

She heard a cough from the porch and turned. John sat on the blanket box, pulling his boots off. He paused a moment to cough again, then pushed his boots into a corner. As she watched, he pressed his hands to his temples, as if holding something in, then straightened. Their eyes met again.

Heather felt the kick of her heart, frustrated that in spite of everything, a mere glance from John could resurrect feelings she thought she'd put well behind her.

"I've got soup ready," she said, walking over to check on the simmering pot.

"I'm not hungry," he said quietly, as he came into the kitchen. "Has Adana had her nap?"

"No. She doesn't seem very tired."

"Good. I'll take her out with me." John stopped as another fit of coughing took over. He hurried to the sink, poured a glass of water and chugged it down. He took another breath, coughed again, then shook his head. "Wish I could get rid of this cold."

Heather was growing concerned about how flushed he appeared. "You look awful."

"I'm fine. I just have to feed the cows. Adana can sit in the tractor cab with me."

"Is that safe?" Why did he want to take her outside when he was obviously not feeling well?

"Your dad rigged up a car seat for her behind the driver's chair. It's plenty safe. The tractor doesn't go that fast."

One look at his red cheeks and watery eyes and Heather's concern was as much for John as it was for Adana. "Maybe not, but I don't think you should be working. You should be in bed. I told you, I can take care of Adana."

"I don't want someone taking care of my daughter who tells her that it's hard to be around her," he muttered.

Heather heard the anger in his voice, saw the puzzled, hurt expression on his face.

Her heart crumpled. He had overheard her comment to his daughter.

She wanted to explain, but how could she do so without revealing everything? She was here for only a short while. She couldn't allow herself to make more than a superficial connection with him.

But as she held his steely gaze, she felt the need to give him something. Some small justification. Anything to take away the judgment she saw on his face, which cut her more deeply than she wanted to admit.

Please help me, Lord, she prayed.

She thought of Sandy, and for a moment hesitated. *Just tell him what he needs to know.*

"You did hear me say that it's hard to be around Adana. There's a good reason." Heather paused, hoping she could do this without breaking down. "I...I was pregnant. Two and half years ago, when Mitch and I were married," she said, her voice hesitant.

"What happened?"

"I lost the baby. She would have been Adana's age." In spite of the time that had passed, saying the words out loud was still painful. "My parents and Keira know, but I asked them not to tell anyone. Even now…it hurts to talk about it."

Heather bit her lip and looked down at Adana again, frustrated at the unwelcome tears that welled up, fighting the emotions that washed over her. "I tried to tell you, that morning when you were working on the fence," she said, her voice breaking. "But I was afraid I would do this." She grabbed a tissue out of the box on the counter, dabbing at her eyes, inhaling deeply as she struggled for control.

"I wish you would have told me," John said, resting his hand on her shoulder. "It would have explained a lot."

His gesture was light, the commiseration of a friend, but the warmth of his fingers, the weight of his palm found the cracks in the barriers Heather had erected to keep her heart safe.

"Sorry. I guess I should have," she said quietly, wiping at tears that, thankfully, seemed to have eased off. "I just didn't want you feeling sorry for me."

"But I do feel sorry for you," he admitted, tightening his grasp on her shoulder. "I know how much I love Adana. To think of losing her…"

His words resurrected the unwelcome tangle of guilt and sorrow that Heather had felt after she'd lost her little girl. She'd wanted a child so badly, but at the same time wanted a better life for her daughter. Something she would never have been able to give any baby she and Mitch might have.

"It was hard, but at the same time…" She faltered. Caught herself. She had to keep some things unvoiced.

Then the phone rang and she rushed to pick it up, grateful for the reprieve. She didn't recognize the caller.

"This is Lisa Abernathy from Fashion Solutions. I'm calling about the application you put in for the job we'd advertised online," the voice on the other end of the line said.

"Good to hear from you, Lisa."

"I'll be in Florida for the next week. I'll give you my number and we can arrange an interview for when I'm back."

Heather grabbed a pen out of the jar her mother always kept handy, and pulled a sticky note off the pad beside it. She wrote down Lisa's number, surprised to see her hands were shaking. She needed this, she realized. A positive step in the right direction.

She and Lisa spoke a bit more about the job and then, with a promise to call, Heather hung up the phone. She put the sticky note on the refrigerator. A solid reminder.

She drew in a deep breath, reminding herself that this was only an interview.

But still…

She turned back to John, who was sitting at the table, Adana on his lap. "That sounded promising," he said.

"It's just an interview. But at least it's not a modeling job."

"Where is it?"

"Atlanta."

"Wow. That's not around the corner."

"I know it would mean moving far away again, but for steady work, I'll go anywhere. Do anything that's an honest day's work."

John nodded.

"You look like you don't approve," she said, folding her arms over her chest.

"It's just that your family misses you," he stated quietly. "I know they would like to have you close by."

"And I'd like to be," she said. "But it's hard to find a decent job in a place like Saddlebank."

"If you could, would you stay?"

She let the idea of living here, close to the ranch, settle in. At the same time, she wondered why John had asked the question. "I might. If I could find a job I liked. Anyhow, that's for tomorrow. Did you want me to put Adana down for a nap?"

"She's not tired. I doubt she'll lie down. Maybe you could take her out for a walk?"

"Good idea." Heather pushed away from the counter just as John got up. He swayed, and she hurried to take Adana from him. "You look horrible," she said, concerned. "Are you sure you don't want to eat, and rest for a bit?"

"I'm not hungry and I can't really rest." He held the back of the chair for a moment. "I should go feed the cows."

"I can help you."

"No. I'll manage."

He didn't look as if he could, but Heather knew better than to try to convince him that he needed help. From past experience, she knew John could be more stubborn than any mule.

So she kept her comments to herself as he walked to the porch, pulled on his boots and left. He paused a moment just outside the house and she saw him bend over and cough.

Then he straightened and glanced behind him, as if he sensed her watching him.

In spite of the fact that the sun was shining on the window and he probably couldn't see inside, she felt suddenly self-conscious.

She shouldn't be staring at him, especially not after she had given him a glimpse into a private part of her life she had hoped to keep secret.

But at the same time, her concern for him overrode her sense of self-preservation. He really looked ill.

John climbed up into the cab of the tractor, pulled the door shut and took a moment to catch his breath. He felt weak and tired. Feeding the cows would take him a lot longer than the hour it usually did, he realized.

Another wave of coughing overtook him. He rode it out, then carefully popped a couple of the cold-and-flu pills he had brought from his house. They usually made him fuzzy-headed, but he didn't care. He needed to get his work done.

When he coughed again, he knew he should have grabbed some of the throat lozenges he'd packed in

Adana's diaper bag. He'd been in too much of a rush to leave, because of the moment he and Heather had shared.

He crossed his arms on the steering wheel and laid his head on them. *Help me stay centered, Lord*, he prayed. *Help me to not get dragged into Heather's life. I'm staying, she's leaving. I have other priorities right now.*

Hadn't he learned from past mistakes?

Fool me once, shame on you. Fool me twice, shame on me. But then he remembered when she'd cried over the baby she had lost. Such a tragedy, he thought, feeling a burst of sympathy. Why hadn't she told him earlier?

It was then that he realized why she hadn't sent him anything after Sandy died. Heather had been dealing with her own loss. Her own heart-wrenching sorrow.

He closed his eyes, his head ringing, his thoughts spinning. Eyes meeting, hands touching... So easily, he recalled the first time he had held hands with her. Their first date. Their first kiss up on the bleachers at a football game.

Then a tapping on the window of the tractor pulled him back to reality.

He looked down from the cab and there she was. Wearing the same old cowboy hat she'd worn when she was helping him with the cows, only now she had Adana on one hip and a travel mug in the other. John rubbed his eyes, trying to get his head back where it should be, then opened the door and leaned down.

Heather held up the mug, its top closed tight. "I

made you some tea with honey," she said. "You didn't have any lunch and I thought it might help your cold."

"Thanks so much," he said, moved by her consideration as he took it from her. "Appreciate it." He set it in the cup holder, then was surprised to see her climb up on the first step leading to the cab.

"Take Adana," she said, handing him his daughter.

"Of course." Disappointment coursed through him, surprising in its intensity. He carefully set Adana in the car seat Monty had rigged up, and buckled her in.

She gurgled in appreciation. "Wide in the tractor. So fun," she babbled.

"Thanks for bringing her," John said, trying not to let his disillusionment seep into his voice.

"Now give me that knife that you use to cut the strings for the bales," Heather said, staying where she was.

He had to shake his head to figure out what she meant.

"It's that orange-handled thing, sitting in that sheath Dad made for it," she said, pointing to a leather holder that Monty had riveted to the opposite door of the tractor.

"What are you…what do you…"

"You're in no condition to do this all by yourself. I'm going to help you."

"What?"

"I know your brain is probably not working at full capacity right now," she said with a teasing smile. "And I'm sure getting in and out of that tractor is going to be exhausting. So if you dump the bales, I'll cut the strings. That way you can stay in the tractor."

"But I can cut the strings."

"I'm sure you can, but I'm not driving the tractor. Especially not with the added responsibility of Adana." Then Heather's eyes grew wide. "And I'm not saying I don't want to be with her. I'm just saying I'm not comfortable with the responsibility. I mean, if something were to happen—"

"It's okay," he said, touching her shoulder to stop her. "I get what you meant."

Her features relaxed. "Okay. Good. So give me that knife and we can get going."

He pulled the knife out of the sheaf, then handed it to her. "I still don't like the idea."

"Well, Adana is all buckled in, which means I've got nothing to do," Heather said with a grin. "So I may as well be productive. Besides, I enjoyed helping you the other day. I'm hoping for another round of adventures and fun."

"If that's what you want to call it."

She grinned again, then slowly climbed down the stairs of the tractor.

Her faithful dog waited, tongue hanging out, obviously looking forward to helping, as well.

John put the tractor in gear but couldn't help watching as Heather walked away from him.

His mind told him to be careful.

But his heart, the one part of him that had never truly stopped loving her, wondered if she would think about staying.

Chapter Eight

"You go to sleep now, munchkin," Heather said, laying Adana in the bed. The toddler's cheeks were red and her eyes had that hazy, unfocused look that signaled sleep was near. Heather felt bad that they had kept her up so long, but she had seemed happy enough in her seat in the tractor.

It was now four o'clock, well past the little one's nap time, and she needed some rest.

Heather pulled the blanket up over Adana's shoulders and tucked it around her. In seconds her eyes drifted shut and her breathing grew heavy.

Heather stood over the crib, trying to separate her own painful memories from this little girl.

It seemed the more Heather saw her, the more time she spent with her, the more the little one charmed her way past the defenses Heather had built. Yes, she reminded her of her lost child and yes, it was painful. But Adana was so cute and so precious that Heather found herself thinking less of her baby and more of Adana herself.

She stayed a moment longer, watching her sleep, listening to her steady breaths. Then she reached down and stroked Adana's cheek, letting this little girl into her heart.

As she did, however, her mind wandered to dangerous territory.

What if she hadn't met Mitch and gone to work for him? What if she had come home from college that horrible year? What if she hadn't been so ashamed of her failures, and realized that she wasn't a student?

Would she and John have stayed together? Had one or two children of their own? Would they be on the ranch, living out their happy-ever-after?

For a few heartbeats, Heather allowed herself to imagine a life with John. With Adana as theirs instead of his.

Then she ran her left hand down her hip, brushing over the small ridged scar on that side. It was only half an inch long. Barely noticeable unless she wore a string bikini, which she preferred not to, for personal and moral reasons.

But it was a reminder of the choices she had made—and their consequences. She couldn't go back in time. She had made her decisions and dealt with the results.

The happy moment with Adana fizzled away like bubbles in a soda. Heather left the room, closing the door quietly behind her.

John hadn't come back yet. She glanced at the clock, quite sure he had said he would return as soon as he parked the tractor. She hoped nothing had happened to him.

She looked out the window and saw the tractor parked just outside the machine shed, still running. Where was John?

Fear rushed through her. She checked back in on Adana, who was fast asleep, then ran to the porch, slid her feet into her ruined leather boots, grabbed a jacket and hurried outside.

When Heather got closer, she still couldn't see John. Her heart was like a block of ice in her chest as she rounded the tractor. John sat in the mud with his back to the huge tire, his knees up, eyes closed.

Heedless of the mud, she dropped to the ground beside him, giving him a shake.

"John. What's wrong?" She shook him again and his eyes flew open.

He blinked, as if trying to assimilate himself to his surroundings, then struggled to his feet. "Sorry. I just felt really tired for a bit."

"How long was a bit?" she asked, helping him to stand.

He tried to shake her off, but she ignored him and slipped one arm around his waist to hold him up. She felt the heat of him even through his jacket. He was burning up with fever.

"I'm okay," he protested.

"No, you are not," she said, ignoring him. "Let's go to the house. Get you cleaned up. You need to get to bed."

"I need to shut the tractor off."

"I'll do that later. Come to the house."

He tried to protest again, but Heather just pulled him along. He stopped fighting and, draping an arm over her shoulder, walked alongside her. "I took something," he said, his voice a croak. "I think I took too much."

Heather's fear melted into surprise. "Took too much of what?"

"Cold medication. I think I read the package wrong."

But as Heather steered him toward the house, she knew that something else was wrong. "You're burning up. I think we should take you to the hospital."

"It's just a cold or the flu," he said, trying to push her away. "They'll just tell me it's a virus and send me home. I'll be better in the morning."

When they finally reached the house, Heather got them both inside. She made him sit on the blanket box while she pulled her own boots off, then bent to remove his.

"Stop," he said. "I can do that."

"I'm sure you can. When you're feeling better. Right now, I think you should have a shower and go to bed."

"I can go to my own house."

"No. I can't keep an eye on you there. And Adana is sleeping right now."

Heather held her hand out to him. To her surprise, he took it, and he didn't let go. He smiled up at her, looking just a bit loopy.

"Thanks for helping me," he said, his voice quiet. "It's been fun being together again. Just like old times. I missed those times. I missed you."

She smiled at him, wondering how much of what he was saying was John and how much was the fever, or the cold medication. Regardless, his words found a home in her soul, settling into the lonely places that had yearned so badly for him, so often.

Then he shook his head, as if he had heard what he'd said. "I'm sorry," he muttered, struggling to his feet. "My head is all muddled. I'll go shower." Then he stopped. "But I don't have any clean clothes."

"I'll run to your house and get some," she said. "I have to turn the tractor off, anyway. I'll be back in a couple of minutes."

He frowned, as if he didn't like the idea of her rifling through his things, then waved his hand. "Sure. That'd be great. I'm going to check on Adana."

John stumbled off, stopping a moment to cough again. Heather heard his footsteps on the stairs, going up to the bedroom where his daughter was sleeping.

She put her boots and coat on again, then jogged across the yard to the tractor. She parked it closer to the shop, turned it off and then went to his house. The door wasn't locked, so she let herself in. A couch and chairs huddled around the fireplace, creating a cozy feeling. She remembered sitting here, playing board games at the table, while John's parents read in the living room.

A perfect home, she thought. She had been happy here. Would she have been happy with John?

The thought lingered just a moment, and again she shook it off. She had no right to allow herself any daydreams where he was concerned. There was no way she could get to where John was; she was weighed down with too much baggage. She had to keep heading in the direction she was going right now.

Away from Mitch and, unfortunately, away from John, who deserved so much more than a mess like her.

She headed down the hallway. The first door she opened was to Adana's room. She guessed John's was the one opposite.

Once inside she made quick work of finding a clean shirt and pants. She folded them up and walked to the dresser to get whatever else he might need. Several pictures on the dresser caught her attention and made her stop.

A photo of Sandy, pregnant, stood off to one side. Adana as a one-year-old, taken in a studio, sat beside it. But it was the other three pictures that surprised Heather.

One of the framed photos was of her and Sandy as young girls, complete with braces and wild hair. They were grinning at the camera. Heather suddenly remembered when that picture had been taken. She'd been invited to Sandy's house shortly after she'd come to the Bannister ranch. They'd had a sleepover, just the two of them.

This must have been part of Sandy's collection, and John, for some reason, had kept it.

Sadness settled over Heather, stirring up memories along with it. Sandy's intervention and subsequent friendship had rescued her from a bleak life with her mother.

Heather didn't deserve to give herself even the smallest space in John and Adana's life. They needed more than she could ever give them.

"I'm so sorry," she breathed, holding the picture, taking a moment to grieve the loss of her friend.

Heather put the picture back, but then another one caught her eye.

It was a large group shot of the Bannister and Fortier kids. Lee, Keira, Tanner, his brother David, John and herself were all mounted on horses, looking like a posse ready to head out and nab bad guys. They were teenagers in the photo, full of hopes and high spirits.

She picked it up, smiling at the sight of all that innocence. So much had happened to all of them, she thought. David had died, Keira had dealt with her own shadows and Lee had gone to jail.

And her?

She put the picture back on the dresser. But as she did, she caught sight of another one. A photo of her alone.

She was on Rowdy, racing around a barrel, hat clamped down on her head, hair flying like a flag behind her. One hand was on the pommel, the other holding the reins as she steered her horse, eyes intent on reading his movements. They were leaning at an impossible angle, clods of dirt airborne behind Rowdy's hooves, looking as if they were suspended in space.

It was one of those rodeo shots taken by the ubiquitous photographers that showed up with their huge cameras at every event, taking pictures and selling them afterward.

Heather didn't remember buying this one. She'd been wearing a shirt she had never particularly cared for—purple silk, with pink sequins and fringe down the arms. She had borrowed it from a fellow rider when her own shirt had ripped.

When had John gotten this and why did he still have it?

Old emotions lingered as she set the pictures back exactly the way they'd been. A quick glance at the photo of Sandy settled Heather's wayward thoughts.

Again she tamped the memories down and grabbed whatever else John might need.

Then, without a backward glance, she left the room.

"I'll be fine," John muttered, though the spinning room and the chills that made his teeth chatter told him otherwise. He thought the shower would warm him up, but he was even colder then before.

"Eventually, yes," Heather said, taking him by the arm and steering him to the room at the end of the main-floor hallway. "For now, you are going to lie down."

"Not in a bed. I'm not an invalid." He pulled away and forced himself to focus as he turned back to the living room. He knew he was being stubborn, but there was no way he was going to bed before the sun went down.

"But you're sick, and you can't argue that away," Heather said. It wasn't hard to hear the exasperation in her voice. "At least lie down on the couch."

John nodded, willing to do that. But he planned on sitting only for a moment. Maybe catching a nap.

Heather grabbed a blanket from her mother's chair as he lowered himself onto the couch.

"I don't need that," he protested.

"You are the worst patient," she declared. "Stop fighting this. Just lie down." She stood above him and he knew that until he laid his head down, she was going to stay there, holding that blanket.

"Okay. But don't let me sleep too long." He swung his feet up and lowered his head to the pillow that Ellen always had sitting at the corner of the couch. He stretched out on the leather sofa, and as he closed his eyes, sleep dragged him down. The last thing he felt was a blanket gently settling on his shoulders, and then he fell into a chaotic dream.

He was chasing cows and Heather was ahead of them. Then the animals veered away and he saw that she had fallen down, was covered in dirt, and was so busy trying to brush it off she couldn't see that the cows were stampeding toward her, snorting and angry. The sun was getting hotter and hotter and he was so thirsty. He had to save Heather, but as he got closer to her, he fell. One of the cows stood over him, breathing on him. He had to get up.

He forced his unwilling eyes open as he dragged himself from a restless sleep.

Something was still breathing on him.

"Sugar, get over here," Heather whispered, and John turned his head to see her dog staring at him, head tilted to one side, mouth open and tongue lolling out, her hot breath bathing John's face.

Relief flooded through him as the border between sleep and wakefulness sharpened and became clear. He gently pushed the dog aside as bits and pieces of the dream rolled through his mind, errant tumbleweeds of thoughts and fear.

"Sorry," Heather said, getting up and shooing

Sugar back onto the porch. "She likes to sneak in when we're not paying attention."

The lights had been turned down, and from what he could see, night had come while he slept.

John tried to sit up as he looked for the grandfather clock in one corner of the living room. He saw that it was nine o'clock.

"Have I been asleep for five hours?" he asked groggily.

"You were sleeping pretty deep," Heather said. "I thought it would be better if you slept as much as possible. Then you started getting restless, but Sugar got to you before I could wake you."

"Had some stupid dreams," he said, struggling to straighten the blankets tangled around him. He rubbed his eyes, feeling remnants of emotions from his dream still clinging like old cobwebs. His fear for Heather. The idea that she needed rescuing. He had never put a lot of stock in dreams, but couldn't shake the idea that part of his dream was true.

He sighed, rubbing his eyes again.

Heather closed the book she'd been reading. "Do you want some tea? Something to eat? You missed lunch and dinner."

"Some tea for now would be great."

She put her book aside, uncurled her long, slender legs and walked past him. He watched her, unable to keep his eyes off her.

"I'm going to heat up some soup for you, as well, just in case you're hungry," she called out as she pulled some containers from the fridge.

"Sure. I'll probably eat it."

"It's cream of potato soup," she said. "I made it this afternoon."

"You always were a fine cook," he said.

"And you're a fine guy for saying exactly the right thing," she returned, her smile blossoming.

As their eyes met, he felt a quieting in his soul. In spite of her high spirits as a young girl, he could always do that to her. Make her smile. Whenever they were together, he felt as if he was exactly in the right place, with the right person.

Then her smile shifted, her expression grew serious and emotions, a blend of old and new, swirled between them.

He wanted to get up, close the space between them and pull her into his arms. Kiss her.

He looked away, massaging his forehead. He wished he could get his thoughts organized. Keep his focus. He thought of his daughter and slowly got to his feet. "I'll go check on Adana," he said.

"She's upstairs. In Lee's old bedroom, across from mine."

The fact that he knew exactly which room had belonged to which Bannister sibling was a reminder of how entwined his life was with theirs, especially Heather.

Adana was fast asleep in the crib, her thumb in her mouth, her bottom in the air. She was wearing sleepers and smelled of shampoo and baby soap. Obviously, Heather had bathed her while he'd slept. The thought made him smile.

John pulled the blanket over her shoulders. "Sleep tight, little one," he whispered.

As he stroked his daughter's cheek, his thoughts drifted to the child Heather had lost. The fact that she'd told him explained so much, and had caused a seismic shift in his perception of Heather's actions around Adana.

And created a measure of sympathy for what Heather had gone through.

Please, Lord, help Heather through this, he prayed. *Comfort her in her sorrow. Help her to find her place in this world.*

As he tried to imagine what that might look like, a small intriguing image lurked around the edges of his mind.

He and Heather and Adana. Here on Refuge Ranch. Together.

He tried to shake that thought off. Heather was just passing through. The phone call she'd taken this morning was a stark reminder of that. He had to be careful and not fool himself, again, into thinking she would choose him over any other plan she was making.

He came back downstairs, clinging to the bannister, disappointed at how shaky he felt. He sank down on the couch again just as Heather brought a tray into the living room.

"You look exhausted," she said. "Are you sure you don't want to go to bed? You can sleep in the room with Adana."

The thought tempted him, but he shook his head. "I'll just eat something and then head back to the house."

"Okay. Sit up and I'll give you the tray. Unless you'd sooner eat in the kitchen."

He glanced toward the table, but the thought of getting up again and walking over there seemed like too much work. Especially when his food was right in front of him.

So he sat up and Heather put the tray on his lap. The soup made his mouth water, but before he picked up the spoon, he bowed his head and prayed a blessing on the food, then prayed again for clear thoughts and direction.

"You still do that," Heather said quietly as she settled in her chair.

"Do what?"

"Pray before you eat."

"You used to, also." In fact, when they were dating they'd often prayed together.

"I did. My faith life has been barren of late."

"In that case, it was good to see you in church on Sunday."

"Felt good to be there. I appreciated what the pastor had to say. That our walls are ever before God. That though we are a work in progress, He is patiently remembering us and working with us. That's…that's a big comfort for me right now." She picked up the book she'd been reading, running her hand along the edge of the pages.

"In what way?"

She just looked at the book, silent, and he wondered if she was going to answer. Then she gazed over at him.

"Like I said, my life has been fragmented." She

spoke tentatively, as if ashamed of what she might be telling him. "It's been kind of messy. A real work in progress, and I'm comforted by the fact that God is guiding me. I just have to trust that everything that happened to me had a purpose." After a moment's pause, she picked up the book she'd been reading and opened it. As if ending that conversation.

John let it lie for now. But he thought of the baby she'd lost and her divorce from Mitch. John didn't want to delve too deeply into her past, since it seemed to hurt her to talk about it, yet at the same time that made him want to know more.

She might be an old girlfriend, but she was still a friend who was hurting. He wanted to help her, but sensed it would have to wait until she was ready to tell him.

"What are you reading?" he asked.

"The Cat in the Hat," she said, giving him a sly grin, a happy glimpse of the old Heather.

Her answer hearkened back to a prank John had played on her when she was in junior high school. Heather didn't like reading, something that Monty and Ellen often complained about. John used to tease her about it. She'd always told him that she would only read books that were short and to the point. So, as a joke, he'd bought a secondhand copy of *The Cat in the Hat* at the library's year-end sale and given it to her.

She'd laughed about it, and next year, for his birthday, she'd given it back to him. It became a running joke between them.

"I won't spoil the ending for you," he retorted.

As he ate, he slowly felt as if his brain was firing on a few more cylinders. "Have you seen the movie?"

"Didn't do the book justice."

He laughed and she lowered her head, back to her book.

But this time the silence held a comfort that surprised him. He finished his soup, set the tray on the coffee table, then picked up the mug of tea she had made him.

"So what are you really reading?" he asked as he leaned back on the couch.

She showed him the cover. "It's called *Reclaiming Peace*."

"I've heard of it. Is that the one about a young girl growing up in Russia?"

"Not the happiest read, but it's compelling." Heather slanted him a curious look. "You seem surprised."

"A bit. From someone who didn't like reading much…"

"I started reading more when I was modeling."

"You had time to read?"

"It's not all posing and walking down runways. There's a lot of time spent waiting for lighting to be set up, having hair and makeup done. Gets tedious at times. A friend lent me one of her books, which I started reading because I was mind-numbingly bored. To my surprise I enjoyed it more than any of the reading I ever did in college."

"I got the idea you didn't enjoy college." He recalled some of the letters she had written to him.

She bit her lip, looking down at her book again,

then slowly shook her head. "I didn't. I never told you, because I was too ashamed, but I didn't do well in college. At all."

John frowned. "I didn't know that."

"It was a hard thing to face," she said, her eyes still on her book. "I had hoped to graduate with something. Some degree. Something that would make you proud of me."

"What do you mean?"

She ran her thumb up and down the edge of the book, as if trying to draw out the right thing to say. "When we were dating, I was always aware of who I was. Where I came from. The pretty girl whose mom was a drunk. I wanted to be more than that for you. I wanted to be deserving of you."

He could only stare at her, as her words settled into his muddled mind.

"But when I was in college, I missed you too much," she continued. "I couldn't study or concentrate. That second year I kind of gave up, and my marks showed it. But Mom and Dad had paid so much for me to go. I felt so stuck. I knew I wouldn't be graduating with a degree, and I couldn't help but feel the weight of responsibility. Then Mitch came around, promising me a job that would pay well. Modeling."

She stopped there, biting her lip, then looked over at John, her eyes holding his. "You were right to warn me about Mitch. I should never have gone with him. I should have told you what was happening in my life."

"Why didn't you?"

Heather pursed her lips, as if still weighing what to say and how to tell him. Finally, she said, "I was afraid. Ashamed." Her eyes held a glint of sorrow. "I should never have broken up with you," she continued. "Never. I'm so sorry. It was the biggest mistake of my life."

He could only stare at her as her words fell into the parched and empty places that his life had been after she'd left Saddlebank. After she'd broken up with him.

As he gazed at Heather, as their eyes met in a long, soul-searching look, he felt the hesitant stirrings of promise. Of hope.

Chapter Nine

As Heather noted John's shocked expression, her mind raced.

Should she have told him? Should she have kept her feelings to herself, when she knew she would be leaving?

But at the same time, she felt as if a load she'd been carrying too long was finally lifted from her shoulders. The past few days she had spent with him reminded her how much she respected John and how dearly she wanted his forgiveness for the mistakes she had made in her life. She wanted to clear things up between them and remove the shadows on their friendship.

Is that the only reason? Could it also have something to do with that photo of you he still has?

She pushed the question away even as her heartbeat quickened. Under John's scrutiny, she felt as if the ground beneath her had shifted, setting her on another path. Though she wasn't sure where she was headed, it seemed now as if she had John at her side.

"So why did you?" he asked. "Why did you break up with me? Was it because of our fight?"

She had started this, Heather reminded herself. She had to finish it.

She folded her hands in her lap and gathered her thoughts. "You need to know where I was at, how I was feeling. I'm not trying to excuse my behavior, but explain it to you."

He was silent, so she continued.

"I had just gotten my midterm grades for my second year and I had failed. Badly. I was so depressed. I knew I wasn't going to pass, which meant I was never going to be a teacher. I felt useless. Through my parents, I had heard about Sandy. How well she was doing and that she was graduating top of her class. That made me feel even more ashamed. Then out of the blue Mitch called me up. There was a career fair that weekend at the college and Mitch said he would be there representing the modeling agency he was interning for. He encouraged me to check it out. So I did. The guy he was with told me that I could have a great career as a model. I didn't tell you at the time, but Mitch and he flew me to New York to meet with the guy's boss the following week. He was excited, and after failing so badly at school, I found it great to hear. I felt like modeling was something that I could do. That I might finally be good at."

"And that's when you signed on with him."

"And that's when you and I had our big fight."

John sighed, pushing his hand through his hair as if he still remembered the awful words they had thrown at each other.

"I'm sorry—"

She shook her head. "No. Don't be. You were right. I should have figured out a way around my problem instead of listening to Mitch. Trouble was, what he offered seemed so much easier than studying harder and taking extra courses, like you suggested. I was afraid if I did what you said, I would fail even more, and I couldn't face that. I'd had enough failures in my life." She drew in a long, slow breath, as if centering herself. Finding her way through this tangle of broken dreams. "Like you warned me, I took the easy way. Trouble was, it didn't turn out to be the easy way."

"What do you mean?"

Too late, she realized that she had ventured too far into waters she'd promised herself she would never stir up again.

"It doesn't matter," she said with a quick shake of her head. "For now, I needed you to know that what we had mattered to me. That I didn't just walk away without regrets." Admitting this seemed to shift what had happened between then and now.

John sighed and laid his head back on the couch, but still gazed at her. "I think all of us live with one type of regret or another. None of us make the right decisions all the time. I think it's a consequence of life."

"Do you have any regrets?" she asked.

He looked up at the ceiling. "Yeah. A few. I regret letting you go as easily as I did. Truth was, I was jealous of Mitch. The first time you two dated, I remember thinking I had missed my chance with you. When he broke up with you, I knew I couldn't wait any longer. Then college happened and Mitch was back in your life. I thought part of the reason you went with him was because you missed him."

John's words were like rocks, falling into the dark pools of her memories.

She was surprised how much it hurt. How much could have changed if they had taken the time to really talk to each other.

"I never missed him. I only went along with his plans because I couldn't see a way around my problem of owing Mom and Dad money."

"They never asked you to repay them."

Heather held John's gaze a moment, realizing that he would never completely understand. What burdens of guilt and obligation she carried, as a child who'd been rescued from her crazy life with her mother.

"I better get that tray back to the kitchen," she said, feeling suddenly breathless. She got up, her book falling to the floor with a thunk.

She picked up his tray, glancing once more at him, but his eyes were closed.

At the sink she busied herself with washing the bowl and utensils. Cleaning the mug. Busy work that kept his words, and the consequences of them, at bay. She had to give herself some time to let the repercussions ease away.

She couldn't let regret eat at her, she thought. She and John had each gone their own way, their lives taking them down diverging paths. She'd had her own goals and, it seemed, he'd had his.

When she could do no more in the kitchen, she returned to the living room. John still sat on the couch, but his face looked more flushed.

"Are you okay?" she asked, concerned. "Do you have a headache?"

"A bit."

She touched his forehead with the back of her hand to check. It was hot, but not burning.

"Do you want me to get you something?"

To her surprise, he caught her wrist, his hand rough on her skin.

"No."

He said nothing more, but didn't let go of her. Slowly, she sat down beside him. Their earlier confessions seemed to have erased the final barriers between them.

"I missed you," he said quietly. "I should have fought for you. Gone after you."

"John…" She breathed his name, not sure if it was a protest or an affirmation.

"I don't want to live with regrets," he whispered.

An invisible force kept their eyes locked on each other, neither able to look away. Past and present melded. Old memories and new. Then he gave her hand a quick tug, his eyes holding the light of promise. She had never been able to resist him.

So she moved closer.

His free hand slipped around her neck, and hers rested on his shoulder.

When their lips met, it seemed the most natural thing in the world. His touch was so familiar it was like finding the dancing partner she had missed all this time. They fit. They belonged.

His lips were warm on hers, and when he kissed her cheek, it was as if he was putting his mark on her.

She tucked her head against his shoulder, her sigh of happiness mingling with the regrets she had given voice to.

"I'm sorry for what happened before," she murmured. It was all she could say.

"I'm sorry, too," he whispered. "I missed you so much."

His words settled the sorrow she had been carrying for so long. "I missed you, too."

He kissed her again, an easy, gentle kiss that created hope.

They sat together for a precious moment, in the here and now. But Heather knew the past would eventually intrude.

It always did.

"So what happens now?" John asked, gently stroking her hair from her face, his movements creating a measure of peace he hadn't felt for a long, long time.

He kept his thoughts resolutely on Heather, his eyes on the fireplace ahead of them. He couldn't look back. He had taken a huge step in a different direction. He had to see this through.

"I don't know." Her voice was quiet, and she rested her hand on his chest.

His head still ached and his mind still seemed fuzzy and confused. But at the same time he felt crystal clear, as if he was exactly where he was supposed to be.

"You still have Adana and I still need to find a job," Heather continued.

He thought of the phone call she had received, and uncertainty marred the moment.

Then he pressed another kiss to her forehead, his arm tightening on her, as if holding back the inevitable. "I shouldn't have asked that question. I'm trying to plan again. To look too far ahead."

"Maybe we'll have to take this one day at a time," she said.

"I'm not used to that," he admitted, laying his cheek on her head. "I've spent too much of my time looking to the future. I've never been able to go with the flow like you. Part of me always admired that."

"Don't admire it too much," she said, with a short laugh. "That was more of a survival skill than a talent."

"From living with your mother?"

Silence followed. Heather had never talked much about life with her mom. It was one of those areas that he had found out was off-limits. He had never pushed, but he also knew that very lack of openness had probably contributed to some of their problems.

She nodded. "I learned never to get too attached to plans because, with my mom, they always changed."

"You never talked about your mother much when we were dating."

She sighed and pulled away from him. She sat back, her arms folded across her chest in a defensive gesture.

"Are you willing to talk about her now?" he pressed.

"Why? That was in the past."

He stifled his annoyance at the stock answer she always gave.

"You never like answering that question, do you?"

She shook her head.

"But your life with your mother is a part of you," he said, keeping his voice calm. Nonthreatening. "I feel as if knowing more about that would help me know more about you."

Again, silence followed his comment. Finally, she lowered her arms and looked at him. "Do we really need to talk about this?"

John held her gaze and slowly nodded. "I think we do. I sometimes think if I had known a bit more, I might have…" He paused there, his eyes holding hers. "Maybe I would have been more patient with you, with some of the decisions you made."

Heather frowned, as if she wasn't going to say anything. Finally, she pursed her lips, her expression serious. Almost cold. "You want to know about my life with my mother? I spent the first ten years hungry. Tired. Sick. My mom would get a job, hate it, quit, spend weeks hanging around whatever furnished apartment, mobile home or motel room we ended up in. We'd get kicked out for nonpayment, move to another town and do it all over again. My mom had guys coming over from time to time. Always someone different. And I went to so many new schools, I can't even remember half of them. I was always teased for my clothes, which were either unsuitable for a girl my age or worn and ragged. When we came to Saddlebank, I expected more of the same. And then I met Sandy. She was one of the few people in my life that saw past all that. One of the few who saw me for who I was." Heather paused, shooting John a quick glance, as if to measure his reaction.

He just smiled at her. "That sounds like Sandy."

"She made all the difference for me. She was the one who told Ellen that I never had lunch when I came to school. She was the one who would invite me over in spite of the fact that her mother didn't really care for me."

John grimaced at that. "What do you mean?"

Heather shrugged. "I think she figured I was an unsuitable friend for her daughter, and given my mom's behavior the few times she was around, when they brought me home, I don't blame Kim for thinking that."

"You really think Kim felt that way about you?"

"Maybe I was oversensitive, but that was the impression I got. Anyhow, when Monty and Ellen took me in, they gave me more than a home. They gave me a measure of self-worth that I never had before." Heather looked suddenly vulnerable. "That was new to me. And I always promised myself that no matter what, I would try to find a way to pay them back. But I didn't know how. And then, when they paid for my education and I failed, I felt even more useless. Then Mitch offered me a way to repay them. With modeling, I'd finally found something I was good at."

"I didn't know you felt that way about the work."

"It felt good to be appreciated and admired instead of constantly feeling like a failure." Heather gave him a wan smile. "But I still should have listened to you."

He caught a plaintive note in her voice, one at odds

with what she'd just told him. "You had other skills," John said softly, thinking of the fight they'd had over the phone. He hadn't even had the opportunity to talk to her face-to-face.

Or to call Mitch out on what he was telling his girlfriend.

"Barrel racing," she said with a faint snort. "That didn't pay the bills the way modeling did. Working in New York helped me find a way to pay Mom and Dad back."

"They didn't need your money, Heather. You know that, right?"

"I know, but I always felt I could never give them enough. Moving in with Monty and Ellen was like moving from murky gray into a world filled with color and light. I always felt as if I owed them."

John's heart hitched and he slipped his arm across her shoulders. "I wish I had known about your struggles," he said. "I wish you would have let me help you."

Heather slowly returned to his embrace, laying her head on his shoulder. "I know. I guess I learned early on in my life that I had to take care of myself, in spite of all that Mom and Dad did for me. I carried that a bit too far, I think."

"I should have come for you," John said, acknowledging his own failings in what had happened. "I should have been more forceful. Tried to talk you out of it."

"I don't know if it would have helped. I felt so deep in this hole that doing what Mitch offered seemed to be the only way out of my dilemma. And it wasn't horrible work at first. I enjoyed dressing up," she said, her voice a low murmur. "And to be honest, seeing myself all made up gave my ragged self-esteem a boost."

John thought of a few pictures that Heather had sent Ellen of the work she had done. He remembered the first time he'd seen her staring at the camera, looking all sultry and smoky-eyed, and he'd realized that the Heather he had loved was as far removed from him as the earth was from the sun.

"I'm sorry that you felt that way," he said. "But you were always beautiful to me, in more ways than just the superficial. You were and are a loving and giving person with a warm heart."

Heather grew very still and he thought perhaps he'd said the wrong thing.

"Thank you. That means a lot to me."

He tightened his hold on her, then pulled her closer, kissing her again.

It felt so good. So right.

"Kissing you is like coming home," he said, tucking her head against his neck once more.

"It's a good place to be," she admitted.

Then they heard Adana cry out, and Heather pulled away.

"I'll go check on her," John said, sitting up, his head suddenly pounding.

"No. You stay here." Heather gently pushed him back. "I'll go see her."

He gave her a slow smile. "Thanks."

Heather left the room and John closed his eyes, surprised at how he could feel so sick and so well at the same time. The glimpses Heather had given him of her life with her mother disturbed him, yet helped him understand why she had done what she did.

"Daddy, I sleep."

Adana's chipper voice made him lift his head. He watched Heather come down the stairs, holding Adana close, her eyes on the steps. When they came toward him, both of them smiling at him, he felt his heart expand.

Could they do this? he wondered. Could they truly sweep away the past years of silence and move on?

He saw Heather's smile widen, and his questions were replaced with hopeful possibilities.

Chapter Ten

"Just take one more bite and then we can go outside," Heather coaxed Adana, who sat in the high chair beside her at the kitchen table.

Early morning sun slanted into the room, illuminating the dancing motes of dust. Sugar, despite Alice's restrictions that she stay on the porch, lay on the rug in front of the kitchen cupboards. Her tail beat out a slow, steady thump of pleasure as she watched Heather and Adana, as if curious to see who would win.

Adana just stared at her, then laughed. "No eat. Go 'side."

Heather looked from the happy girl to the bowl of porridge she had been trying to feed her. Adana had eaten about a third of it. Was that enough?

"How about one more mouthful?" she asked, not sure if she should push her.

Adana turned her head aside and held her chubby hands out in front of her in a classic gesture of denial.

"Okay. I'm not going to be the big meanie,"

Heather said, dropping the spoon in the bowl. She took the leftovers to the sink, walking around Sugar, who dropped her head on her paws, obviously losing interest in the standoff.

"Do you think I should have pressed her?" Heather said to the dog as she rinsed out the bowl. "Am I too much of a pushover?"

Sugar just looked up at her, then laid her head on her paws again and eased out a doggy sigh.

"You're no help," Heather said as she put the bowl in the dishwasher, then went back to get Adana and set her on the counter beside the sink. As she rinsed out a cloth to wipe the toddler's face, she glanced out the window and her hands grew still. She let her gaze drift past the barns and corrals to the rolling hills surrounding the ranch. The snow was completely gone now and soon, with the spring rains, the fields would be greening up.

Her soul felt nourished, revived by the open land, and she tested the idea of staying. Could she find a job in Saddlebank that would allow her to feel independent? That would give her the sense of self-worth she'd spent so much time seeking?

"Daddy, coming here," Adana called out, scrambling to her feet to stand on the counter, pressing her hands against the window.

Heather steadied her as she watched John walk toward the house. As a concession to the warmer weather, he wore a faded denim jacket instead of a coat over his shirt. His gloves were tucked in the back pocket of his blue jeans. His worn cowboy hat was pulled low over his face, but as Heather watched, he paused to cough again. Last night he had slept at his own house and she hadn't seen him yet this morning.

As she studied him, she felt her heart shift in her chest. This man had taken up so much of her thoughts. And for a bleak time in her life she'd thought she would never see him again. Never be a part of his life.

Now?

She allowed herself a wisp of a dream. She and John and the little girl beside her. Together. The thought swirled through Heather's mind, and for an enticing moment it solidified.

Could she and John recapture what they had once had?

He was closer by now and looked toward the house. He saw them and waved, and Adana wiggled her chubby fingers back at him. "Daddy. Come," she called out, the imperious tone in her voice making Heather laugh.

"You are a little princess, aren't you," she said.

She set Adana back down, turned her face with a gentle hand and carefully wiped her mouth, cheeks and hands. Adana allowed her to do so, then smiled up at her.

Heather's heart swelled as she looked down at the little girl. This adorable child had slowly worked her way into her heart. She hadn't wanted to fall in love with her. Would have preferred not to. She was such a clear reminder of what Heather had lost, but slowly Adana had taken on her own personality. Adorable and precious.

Heather set the cloth down and picked the child up in her arms. To her surprise, Adana laid her head in the crook of Heather's neck and wrapped her own arms around her.

"Love you," she said.

Heather choked back a sob and clung to her, pure love washing over her.

"You little munchkin," she whispered, pressing a kiss to her forehead, as tears threatened. "You darling little girl."

She gently rocked Adana in her arms. She couldn't cry. She couldn't start that. She squeezed her eyes tightly shut, dismayed to feel a tear slip down her cheek.

"Hey, are you okay?"

She startled as she felt John's hand on her shoulder. She quickly averted her head, surreptitiously wiping at the moisture on her cheek. "I'm fine," she said with forced cheerfulness, giving herself a second to compose herself. She shifted the child in her arms, still looking away. "I was just cleaning Adana up from breakfast. She didn't have much to eat, I'm afraid. I wasn't very strict with her so she'll probably be hungry in an hour or so."

Stop now. You're babbling.

When Heather felt she finally had her emotions under control, she turned back to John.

He was watching her, a curious look on his face.

"So, how are you feeling?" she asked, trying to avert the questions she saw in his eyes. She had told him so much already, she felt raw from the exposure. She needed to retrench, find her footing and keep her head on straight.

John wagged his hand. "A bit good and a bit not

so good." He coughed again, as if underlining his comment.

"What's on the agenda today?"

"Not a lot. Cows are processed and the fences look good. I thought you and Adana might want to take a drive into town with me. I have to get some oats for the horses and some oil for the tractor. It needs an oil change. We could stop at the Grill and Chill for a cup of coffee after I get what I need."

That seemed so domestic. Going into town with John and Adana.

"As long as we're home after lunch," Heather said. "Keira and Tanner are back this afternoon and she really wanted to go for a ride."

"We'll be back by then."

"Great. That would work out fine. I should pick up a few things for the bridal shower on Thursday, as well. I told Keira that since I was around, I would do some baking for it."

"That's right. That's coming up. I forgot."

"Keira will be so disappointed that this very important event is not on your social calendar," Heather teased.

John's grin settled into her soul. She drew in a slow, deep breath and then took a step closer and brushed a kiss over his cheek. He smelled of soap and horses and the outdoors.

He smelled like John.

"Do you need breakfast?" she asked as she stepped back, a sudden blush warming her own cheeks.

"I'll just grab some juice and an apple," he said, giving her a warm smile. "I'm not really that hungry."

"Are you sure? You're not going to get better if you don't eat."

John's expression grew serious and he cupped her jaw with a callused palm. "I feel better already."

Their eyes held a moment, then Adana tried to wriggle free, making her presence known. "Go 'side," she insisted.

"I guess her majesty is letting us know what she wants," Heather said, jiggling her. "Give me a few moments to change her, get a diaper bag together and make up a grocery list, then we can go."

"I can change her," John said, reaching out to take his daughter.

"That's okay. I know where everything is. I don't mind."

John looked at her as if to make sure, then gave her another one of his slow-release smiles that could always melt her heart, and stepped back. "I'll gas up the truck and meet you outside."

Fifteen minutes later Adana was safely buckled in her car seat and Heather was buckling up herself. "Can we stop at the mechanic and check on my car?" she asked as John turned the ignition on the truck. "The last time I talked to Alan, he still hadn't received the part, but he said he hoped it would be in this week."

"Of course. Hopefully, it will be ready soon."

Heather nodded. The outside world was intruding into this little bubble she and John seemed to have created in the past few days. Her thoughts shifted to the phone call offering her an interview.

She glanced at John, who was looking ahead as he

drove from the ranch, to Adana, who was watching her as if curious about her decision. Could Heather dare think that things had progressed so far between her and John that she could change her plans?

A shiver of fear ran through her even as the idea created anticipation. Both Mitch and her mother had taught her hard lessons on taking care of herself. The importance of not being dependent in anyone.

But Monty and Ellen had shown her how life in a family and a community worked. How people could help you. Support you.

And John? Where did he fall?

"So, where in town did you want to go first?" he asked, breaking into her thoughts.

"Doesn't matter," she said. "Why don't you do what you need to first, so we can get groceries just before we leave."

"And we can hurry home if you buy ice cream," he joked.

Heather laughed. "I remember many a rushed trip back from town on hot summer days, with a pail of ice cream sitting in the back of the truck melting. Mom always said she wasn't going to buy ice cream, but gave in when Lee would turn his big brown eyes on her."

"He had even more pull than you did," John said with a laugh.

Heather grew serious again, thinking of her brother, now away from the ranch. "I hope he's doing okay. I heard he didn't come back for Thanksgiving or Christmas."

"You're not the only prodigal child," John said quietly.

"I'm sure it's been hard for Mom and Dad," Heather said. "Having kids leave and not come back."

"We certainly can't plan our children's lives," John stated.

Heather nodded, glancing over at Adana. "It's different when you're a parent; isn't it? You're pretty vulnerable. They hold so much of your heart."

The two-year-old was staring straight ahead, as if lost in her own little world. Feeling a slow swirl of love, Heather put her hand on the little girl's leg, her fingers brushing John's in the process, creating a connection between them, as if completing a circle.

He twined his fingers through hers and squeezed gently. "I'm sorry for you. I'm sorry it's hard to be around Adana."

Heather shook her head. "It isn't. Not anymore. She's so precious."

"That means a lot to me. That you feel that way about her."

"It's not hard to," Heather said, gazing down at Adana who, at that precise moment, looked up at her and grinned. "Yes. I'm talking about you," she said with a gentle laugh, touching her chubby cheek.

This little girl had wormed herself into her heart. A heart that her father seemed to be making inroads on himself.

But could she open herself up to him again, make herself vulnerable?

And would he do the same?

* * *

"Are you ready for some coffee and pie?" John asked as he drove past the park with its white gazebo and onto Main Street. The trees were still bare, but the park grass was slightly green. A promise of summer coming.

"We may as well. The mechanic won't be open until after lunch."

"And we haven't bought your ice cream yet," John said as he parked his truck. He pulled the keys out of the ignition and glanced over at Heather who was already unbuckling Adana from the car seat between them.

Heather's quick laugh brushed, featherlight, over his soul. It was a good sound. One he hadn't thought he'd ever hear again. "I haven't had ice cream in ages," she admitted.

"I don't imagine it's on the menu for models," he said with a grin as he reached for Adana.

But the fickle child twisted away from him. "No. Go wif Hevver," she insisted.

"Sorry," Heather said, but as she took the little girl in her arms, John could see that she didn't mind at all. So he grabbed the diaper bag, feeling a bit like a porter.

"Town is busy today," he said, slipping the bag over his arm as they walked down the street.

"It's the sunshine," Heather said, lifting her face to the bluebird sky. "Makes everyone want to get outside."

"Enjoy it while you can. There's rain in the forecast."

"Springtime in Montana," Heather murmured. She sighed happily as she looked around town. "I missed this place," she said. "I missed the brick buildings and the wide streets and knowing half the people here."

"There's brick buildings in New York," John teased.

"Forty stories tall," Heather returned. She nodded at a woman who smiled at them, and for a moment John wondered how they looked to passersby. A man and a woman with a little girl.

A family unit.

A bite of sorrow hit him suddenly. He and Sandy had never shared moments like these. She hadn't had the joy of seeing Adana change and grow.

"You okay?" Heather asked. "You want to go home? You look a little peaked."

"I'm fine."

"Are you sure?" she pressed.

John held her concerned look, thinking of what she had told him. How it had made him feel connected to her. He could do no less.

"To tell you the truth, I'm thinking of Sandy right now. How she never got to hold Adana like you are now."

Heather stopped in her tracks, looking upset as she tried to give Adana back to him. "Oh, no. I didn't mean to take her place. It's just Adana…"

John dropped a reassuring hand on her shoulder. "Sorry. I was just sharing my thoughts. Kind of like you did." He shrugged, feeling as if he had messed things up. "Sandy always told me I needed to be more diplomatic."

Heather held his gaze, then her smile broke out again. "That's okay." She looked from him to Adana. "I guess it's just a little tricky yet. For both of us."

John thought of Monty's veiled warning, and the possible repercussions of what he knew was growing between him and Heather. For now, he simply had to let things go.

"In some ways it can be tricky, but in others it feels like the most natural thing in the world."

Heather's smile grew. "That means a lot."

John squeezed her shoulder, then brushed a wisp of Adana's hair out of her eyes, glad he had told Heather what he did. "You need a haircut, missy," he said, covering up his momentary self-consciousness.

Heather agreed. "I was thinking of trimming her bangs, but wasn't sure you'd be okay with it."

"When we get home you can do it."

"It's a date," she said.

"Let's go see what Gord has to offer today at the Grill and Chill."

John pulled open the door of the café, and the cheerful hum of conversation, the clink of silverware and the occasional shout of laughter washed over them.

Allison Bamford, the owner's sister and part-time waitress, bustled past them, an empty coffeepot in one hand, a tray of dirty dishes in the other, her blond ponytail bobbing with every step. "Your parents are on the lower level," she called out to John. "There's plenty of room with them."

John looked around at all the full tables, not seeing any other option.

"Is that okay with you?" he asked Heather.

"Of course. I haven't seen your parents in ages."

John worked his way among the crowded tables, then down three worn stairs to the lower level of the coffee shop, which had been added about ten years ago. He glanced around, then caught sight of his father's balding head just beyond a crowd of young people at a long, rectangular table. Beside him sat John's mother, her glasses pushed high on her head, messing up her short, graying hair. She was smiling at her husband, her gray eyes crinkling at the corners.

His dad looked up and caught John's attention. He waved them over with an exaggerated sweep of his arm.

But as he and Heather approached, John found his steps faltering. Across from them, at a table for six, sat Sandy's parents, Kim and Rex Panko. Kim, a petite brunette, looked as stylish as ever, with some kind of gauzy scarf wrapped around the shoulders of her pink dress. Rex looked like he always did. Golf shirt, khaki pants and a windbreaker embroidered with the name of his favorite hockey team.

This was unexpected. John had thought Kim and Rex were going to be out of town for at least another day. They hadn't called to let him know they were back.

He wasn't sure he wanted Sandy's parents to see him with Heather. Not when things were very precarious between them. Their relationship was too fragile for the scrutiny of his parents, let alone his in-laws.

"Hey, John," his father called out, waving him

over. "And our little Adana. This is a pleasant surprise."

Too late to back out now.

His mother jumped to her feet, gave him a quick hug, then looked past him to where Heather stood with Adana. John caught the puzzlement in her expression and felt suddenly self-conscious.

"Um, you remember Heather Bannister," he said, shooting a quick glance at her. She held back, appearing clearly distressed. "Heather's home at the ranch for a couple of weeks. Helping Keira with her bridal shower. She's the maid of honor." He stopped his nervous chatter, aware that his father was looking at him with curiosity. His parents knew his history with Heather too well.

And he knew that they knew. It was going to be an uneasy few moments. Maybe they could stay for a cup of coffee and then use the excuse that Adana needed a nap to make a quick getaway.

"Of course I remember. Come, sit down," his mother said, pushing out the chair beside her. "Hello, Heather. Wonderful to see you again."

"Good to see you, too, Paige," she replied, shifting Adana on her hip.

"And our little muffin." John's mom leaned closer and gave her granddaughter a kiss. "Good to see you, sweetie."

"Hi, Nana," Adana said, grinning at her.

"Hey, baby girl," Sandy's mother said, also getting up, arms extended. "Come sit with Granny. I missed you so much."

But to John's consternation, Adana shook her head, clinging to Heather. "No, fank you."

"Oh, come on, honey. Granny hasn't seen you for almost a week." Kim moved closer, grabbing Adana under the arms as if to take her from Heather. But the toddler pulled away, waving her hand at Sandy's mother. "Don't want to see Gammy," she cried out.

Kim's features seemed to crumple.

"Go to your granny," Heather cajoled her, positioning her for the transfer.

"No. No. Stay wif Hevver." Adana curled her arms around Heather's neck, and a distinctly uncomfortable silence fell.

"Well, this is an interesting development," Kim finally said, sitting down, her arms crossed so tightly across her chest that John was surprised she could breathe, let alone speak.

Oh, boy.

Sandy's mother could be very proprietary where Adana was concerned. John had to make sure he kept the visits between Sandy's parents and his own equally balanced. It was exhausting at times.

"And what brings you to town?" he asked as he held a chair out for Heather, trying to find a way to break the silence that held everyone around the table in an awkward grip.

"Just wanted to get out," his father said. "Treat your mother to some of Gord's famous pie."

"John, you sound like you're coming down with a cold," his mother said.

"Actually, just getting over it. I feel a lot better today than I did yesterday."

"You make sure you get enough rest." His mom gave him a gentle smile. "You've been pushing yourself way too hard lately."

"Spoken like a typical mother," he said, sending another concerned glance Heather's way, wondering how she was doing. She sat like a statue, her expression neutral, but John could see faint lines of tension bracketing her lips.

Allison stopped by, setting menus in front of them on the crowded table.

"I'll just have coffee," John said, glancing at Heather and raising his eyebrows.

"The same for me," she said. He didn't think he imagined the relief on her face when she realized they'd be there for only a short time.

"What about Adana?" Kim was asking. "Shouldn't she have something to eat?"

"I gave her a banana and some yogurt while John was at the machine shop," Heather said. "And she just finished a whole juice box."

"Is that enough?" Kim pressed.

Heather shot him a quick look, as if asking for backup.

"That's all she usually eats," John said. "She'll be fine."

Kim looked as if she was about to say something else, but then, thankfully, his mother jumped into the conversation.

"So, Heather, how are plans for the shower coming? Is there anything I can do to help?"

"They're coming well, and thanks for the offer. I have to buy a few things. I'm doing some baking.

Mom is picking up some decorations in Missoula. She and Dad are coming home tonight, as are Keira and Tanner."

"So you two are alone at the ranch? Where's Alice?" Kim again.

John almost cringed at her tone of voice, the sight of her pursed lips and narrowed eyes. For some reason, Kim had directed her question at Heather, but he chose to answer.

"When Alice found out that Heather was home for a while, she decided to go visit her aunt. She's not doing well, apparently."

Kim's slow nod felt more like a judgment than an acceptance of the facts.

At that moment Allison returned with a pot and poured them cups of coffee. She refilled the rest, then left again.

"And how are things at the ranch?" John's father asked, changing the conversation.

"Good. Heather and I got all the precalving shots done." John eagerly jumped on that safer topic as he spooned sugar into his coffee. "Fences are all up to snuff. We need some good spring rain to get the frost all the way out of the ground before the pastures green up."

"Cattle prices are good," Rex Panko chimed in, giving John a quick grin. "And that's all I know about cows." He turned to John's dad. "Have you got your greenhouse going?"

"Of course. I've already got my Aspermums started and the cucumbers are doing well."

John took a sip of coffee, glancing at his watch

and wondering how long they had to sit there before it was polite to leave. Once his father got started on his plants and flowers and plans for the yard, he could go on for hours.

His mother asked Heather some questions about Keira's wedding. Safe topics, John thought, his attention mostly on Heather. She didn't look very comfortable and he suspected it had something to do with Kim.

"Will you be seeing your natural mother on this visit?" he heard Kim ask.

John knew he shouldn't eavesdrop, but her comment about Heather's mother caught his attention.

"I don't know where she is," Heather said quietly. "We haven't talked in years."

"I thought I saw her in Bozeman last time we were there," Kim was saying. She turned to her husband, putting his hand on her arm. "Didn't we see Beryl, Heather's mother, there, Rex? When we went to that play?"

Rex shot her a puzzled look. "I…I don't know. Can't remember."

"I'm sure we did. I thought I saw her at that pub, the Iron Horse. She looks just like you. Same slim figure, long blond hair and blue eyes."

"Sounds like you could be describing about a quarter of the female population in Bozeman," John said with a forced laugh. He wasn't sure he liked the way Kim was talking.

She gave him a tight smile. "Maybe, but I always thought that Heather and her mother looked so much the same. There were so many similarities between them they could have been sisters."

John tried to figure out why she was doing this. Kim wasn't always the warmest person, but she wasn't vindictive. It seemed she was determined to remind Heather of her humble beginnings.

"Heather, what are your plans when your visit is over?" his mother was asking, breaking into the conversation. "Ellen told me you're only here for a short while. She's very sad about that."

"I know, but I need to get to work," Heather answered.

"I just heard that Seth over at the Feed and Seed is looking for someone to head up his tack and saddle division," his father said. "You always were pretty knowledgeable about that sort of thing."

"And didn't Marnie say something about looking for someone to run training clinics?" his mother mentioned. "For barrel racing. Your old specialty. You were one of the best. You could easily do this."

"Sounds like fun," Heather said with a faint smile. "I miss working with horses."

"I could tell her you're interested."

"I do have a job interview in Atlanta," Heather said with a thoughtful frown. "But it's not for a week or so. I could talk to Marnie."

The fragile hope that had been stirring in John's heart grew with Heather's last comment.

"This job interview, is it for your modeling work?" Kim asked.

"No. Office work. But still related to fashion."

"I find it so interesting that you ended up in that

field," Kim continued, toying with the salad in front of her. "I know Sandy was never the slightest bit interested in clothes or makeup."

"She liked dressing up sometimes," John said, again puzzled by Kim's attitude.

"Maybe, but Sandy had other priorities," her mother said with a smile. "Like her studies."

"Sandy was a very smart girl. And she had a good heart. I was very lucky to have her as a friend." Heather's voice grew quiet. Then she looked over at John, her expression pensive. "And John was blessed to have her as a wife."

John was pleasantly surprised at how diplomatically Heather deflected Kim's comments and turned the conversation back to a positive note. "I *was* blessed," he agreed, giving Heather a grateful smile. "I think anyone who knew her was."

Heather returned his smile, then gently removed the napkin Adana had been shredding with her sticky fingers. "Don't play with that, honey," she said. "Let me get you a toy."

"I'll get it for you," John said, reaching for the diaper bag hooked over the back of his chair the same time Heather did. Their fingers brushed and for a moment he surreptitiously caught her hand, giving it a squeeze of encouragement.

"I'm so sorry," he whispered as he bent his head to pull a toy out of the diaper bag, hoping she understood what he was apologizing for.

"It's fine," she whispered back, her returning smile showing him that she understood.

He found a small giraffe squeeze toy that Adana

was especially fond of at the bottom of the bag. But as he handed it to his daughter, he caught Kim looking from him to Heather.

As if she knew what was happening.

And she didn't look pleased.

Chapter Eleven

"Sorry about that," John said as they walked back down the street to where his truck was parked. "I didn't think my parents would be there, let alone Sandy's mom and dad."

"It's okay," Heather assured him, still holding Adana. She had tried not to let the comments Sandy's mother made get to her.

Seeing Sandy's parents had been harder than she'd expected it would.

When Heather was younger and would visit Sandy at her home, Kim had been unfailingly polite, but Heather often got the feeling that she didn't approve of her. It didn't seem as if that had changed. Adana's rejection of Kim in favor of her probably didn't help matters any.

"It was good to see your parents again," Heather said as John unlocked the truck and opened the door for her. "Your mom hasn't changed a bit."

"Still as spunky as ever," John said. "Her and dad

still put in a huge garden. They give half of it away, though."

"Does your dad miss being on the ranch? I can't imagine him living in town." Heather placed Adana in her car seat and quickly buckled her in.

"I think ranching for him was just a job. He loved working for your dad, but he likes being retired even more. And he seems to have found his passion in raising flowers."

"But he was a really good ranch hand and foreman," Heather said, surprised at the comment. "My dad always said he could never have found someone better."

"He was. It just wasn't his life's dream."

"Is it yours?"

John shrugged as he got into the truck. As he turned on the ignition, he slowly shook his head. "Is it my dream to be a hired hand? No. I have other plans."

"What plans?"

John rested his hands on the steering wheel as if weighing what he was going to say. Then he turned to her. "You may as well know. Just before you came back, I gave your dad a proposal. To buy into the ranch. As a partner."

Heather could only stare at him. "A partner with my father? Why?"

"He's getting older, and it doesn't look like Lee is coming back. Your dad is going to need a working partner fairly soon. And I'm not content to be a permanent hired hand, like my father was."

Heather blinked, trying to absorb this information.

"But Refuge Ranch has been in my father's family for decades."

"I know. But I also know that your dad can't keep running it on his own, and like I said, I have plans." He stopped there. "I want you to know this because of our history, and because I feel like things are changing between us. When you came back last week, your father warned me to be careful with you. And I wanted to be. I had my own plans, my own focus. I didn't want you to be a distraction." He reached past his daughter and touched his finger to Heather's cheek, letting it linger a moment, then drift to her chin.

"I'm sorry if I was," she said, suddenly breathless.

"I'm not."

It was quiet for a moment as unspoken expectations thrummed between them. A glimpse of a future she wasn't sure she dared allow.

Then Adana grabbed at John's hand. "Go, Daddy. Go," she said, and the moment disappeared.

But as John put the truck in Reverse, he glanced at Heather again, and she knew that remnants of what they had just experienced still lingered.

Her thoughts were a confused whirl of maybes and what-ifs. John buying into Refuge Ranch. Making plans for permanency. Did she dare make herself dependent again? When she'd left Mitch, she'd promised herself that from then on, her focus was going to be on taking care of herself and putting her own needs first.

But when John beamed at her, she felt a sense of coming home. A sense of hope.

"I think we can make this work," he said quietly.

She felt a smile begin in her soul and spread to her face. "I think we can, too."

Then, as John backed into the street, Heather saw Mr. and Mrs. Panko coming down the sidewalk. As they drew closer, Rex waved, but Kim clutched her purse, her smile seemingly forced.

The old misgivings, the old feelings of unworthiness set in. Kim could always do that to her.

Heather and John might have hopes and dreams, but there were other people to be considered. And she highly doubted that Kim would give her blessing.

"So, grocery store next?" John asked as they headed down the street.

Heather pulled herself back into the moment. "Yes. That would be good." She reached for her purse and found her shopping list, reading over the mundane items as if to center herself.

Make a plan and stick to it.

She suddenly felt as if she were working her way through a dark passage, unable to see what was directly in front of her.

Help me make the right decision, Lord, she prayed as she shoved the list back into her purse.

She closed her eyes, unclenching her hands as if trying to find out what that decision was.

"You okay?" John's voice broke into her thoughts, and as her eyes met his, she felt a peace flow through her. She would figure this out, she told herself.

"Yes, I am," she said, forcing a smile.

"We can stop at the garage first and find out what's going on with your car," he offered.

"Sounds good."

"Did you want to stop in to talk to Marnie at the Seed and Feed? About the barrel-racing clinic she wants to start up?"

"I'll call her when I get home."

"Of course," he said.

Heather hated seeing the hope in his eyes fade away, but she had to find her footing before she headed in a different direction than originally planned.

One step at a time, she reminded herself. One step at a time.

An hour and a half later they were turning down the road leading to the ranch, groceries safely stowed in the back of the truck. Adana was fast asleep, her head drooping to one side.

"I feel bad that we have to wake her up when we get to the ranch," Heather said as she carefully righted her head.

"She'll be okay," John said. "I've come back from town many times and had to wake her up to move her to her crib, but she always falls right back asleep."

"I hope so," Heather said with a yawn, the thrum of the tires and the warmth of the cab lulling her. "I used to hate it when my mother would wake me up and I'd have to walk from the car to the apartment or hotel. I almost always fell somewhere along the way."

"I take it you're talking about your natural mother."

Heather felt a flush heat her cheeks. She didn't like speaking about her life with Beryl. Somehow her comment had just slipped out. She supposed it had something to do with what Kim had said about her. As if she was determined to remind Heather of where she came from.

It wasn't fair of Heather to make that assumption. Kim had known her first as Beryl's daughter, not as Monty and Ellen's.

"Yeah. I was. Bit of déjà vu."

"What do you mean?"

Heather stifled the usual shame and guilt that surrounded any talk of her mother. "Kim always brought up my mother when I was around her. She always made me feel so confused about who I am."

"How so?"

Heather couldn't help but think of the two couples they had just sat with. Sandy's and John's parents. Both still married to each other. Both married, period. A legacy of love and fidelity that wasn't part of Heather's own history.

"Beryl was my mother, I know, but she wasn't a good one, and I really struggle with my feelings toward her. I told you part of what it was like. I also spent a lot of time hungry. Many nights I slept in the backseat of a car, while we were driving from one town to another, or were parked outside of a bar. I was always ashamed of her and ashamed of my life because of what she would do." Heather stopped there, tamping down the memories. "Monty and Ellen saved my life and showed me how a family works. But now and again I catch myself wondering how much of my mother is in me. How many of my choices came from her."

John covered Heather's hand with his. "You are not your mother. You are your own person. You made your choices from a different place than she did. You've had Monty and Ellen giving you guidance."

Heather considered his words, but wondered if she could believe them entirely. If she could completely escape her mother's legacy. She looked at Adana, Sandy's daughter. The little girl had managed to find a place in Heather's heart.

As she gazed back at John, the feeling hit her with devastating simplicity.

She wanted to be with him. She wanted to be with Adana.

But right on the heels of that thought came Kim's judging looks. The feeling that no matter how hard Heather tried, she would always be her mother's daughter. Heather tried to hold back the thoughts, but they made their way into her mind, and with them came memories of Mitch.

How he used to taunt her with the idea that she was just like her mother. How he used to make her feel as if she could never be good enough.

"See I have engraved you in the palms of my hands. Your walls are ever before Me."

The words from church on Sunday erased the hurtful memory.

But it couldn't completely eliminate the feeling that she wasn't worthy. Maybe she was fooling herself, she thought, looking out the truck's window.

She closed her eyes, pressing her lips together. *Forgive me, Lord*, she prayed. *I'm not worthy to be a part of John's life. To be any kind of mother to Adana.*

They topped the rise, then headed down the driveway to the ranch house. To her surprise, Monty's and

Tanner's trucks were parked in front of it. They were back earlier than she thought they would be. And as John pulled up beside them, Heather felt as if reality had intruded along with the unexpected return of her family.

John parked the truck and she unbuckled Adana. Then he got the groceries out of the back.

John carried the plastic grocery bags as she climbed out, holding Adana close. As he had promised, the little girl simply laid her head on her shoulder and was already asleep again.

"Told you," he said. "She'll pop back to sleep when you lay her in the crib."

As they approached the house, the door opened and Keira came out, laughing, looking back over her shoulder at Tanner, who was right behind her. She stopped short, Tanner almost running into her. Keira's green eyes flicked from John to Heather, a mischievous smile crooking her mouth as if she guessed what had happened while they were gone. "So, you're back from wherever it was you went."

"And you're back early." Heather hoped she didn't sound as disappointed as she felt.

"The show wasn't as good as we thought it would be so we left this morning. Where did you go?"

"John drove me to town to check on my car and get groceries for the shower," Heather explained, refusing to rise to the question she saw in her sister's eyes. "I thought I would make that lemon pound cake that you like, and turtle cheesecake squares. And I picked up some tissue paper to make some of those puffy balls to hang from the ceiling."

She hoped talk of the shower would sidetrack Keira, but her sister was still grinning, obviously not distracted by Heather.

"Tanner and I were thinking of taking the horses out. It's a bit cold yet, but the fields are bare and I need to get out after being cooped up in the truck all week. You said you were going to come. Do you think John will join us?"

Heather couldn't stop the lift of her heart at the thought of riding Rowdy out in the hills with John.

And yet she felt a measure of reluctance. "I don't think so. Someone has to watch Adana, and Alice isn't back yet."

"Dad can help Mom watch her," Keira said. "Looks like Adana will sleep most of the afternoon, anyhow."

"I'll stay behind," John said, giving Heather an encouraging smile. "You go. You'll love it."

"You should come, too, John," Tanner interjected. "You said you wanted to work Clyde. Be a good time to see how he handles."

John wavered, then Keira took the bags from his hands. "I'll put these away and tell Mom and Dad that they're babysitting."

"Are you sure it'll be okay?" John asked.

"Go already. Heather and I will join you at the corrals."

"Okay. I'm not going to argue with a Bannister woman."

Heather tried to catch John's eye, but he and Tanner were already walking away, talking.

Keira was headed inside the house. Heather followed her, holding Adana, determined to do the right thing, but so tempted by the thought of riding with John.

Keira set the grocery bags on the kitchen counter and started putting them away. "Hello, darling," her mother said as she got up to help. "How did you make out while we were gone?"

"Don't ask," Keira said with a twinkle.

"What does that mean?"

"She means nothing," Heather said, tossing her sister a warning glance. "How was your visit with the specialist?"

"Went well. He said I'm showing good improvement."

"Gad to hear that. I'm going to put Adana in her crib." She brushed a quick kiss over her mother's cheek, gave her father a wave of greeting and hurried up the stairs to the room where Adana usually slept.

Heather carefully laid the girl down and covered her with the quilt, tucking it around her body. She smoothed Adana's hair back from her face, a mixture of emotions swarming through her. Questions piling on top of hopes. Could she be the person John needed? Did she dare think that a relationship with him was in her future?

Her hands clung to the rail of the crib as she looked down at the sweet child, thinking of what John had told her. The promise he had made that he would take care of this helpless child. No matter what.

Help me do the right thing, Lord, she prayed. *For John and Adana.*

Because right about now she wasn't sure what the right thing was.

She quietly left the room, and as she came down the stairs, Keira called out to her.

"Mom and Dad don't mind taking care of Adana, just like I figured. Meet us at the corrals in ten minutes. Don't be late."

Heather hurried down the stairs to stop her, but Keira was already out the door.

"You look a little flushed, honey," her mother said, as she carefully rolled up the plastic bags to be reused. "Are you feeling okay?"

"I'm fine," she quickly returned. "What did the specialist say about your collar?"

Her mom sighed and sat back in the chair as Heather's dad gave her a quick kiss hello, then picked up some of the cans to put away.

"I'll be wearing it for at least another month. So disheartening. The break isn't setting as quickly as he had hoped. But at least it's getting somewhere. How were things here while we were gone?"

Was it Heather's imagination or was her mother looking at her a little too keenly? With a little too much expectation? What had Keira said to her?

"John wasn't feeling well, so not a whole lot."

But Heather couldn't help stealing a glance toward the living room, where she had opened her heart to John. Where they had shared a kiss.

Where things had changed between them.

"Cows got fed?" Monty asked as he returned to the table empty-handed.

"Yes. Because John wasn't feeling that well, I helped him the one time."

"Good." Monty paused a moment, watching her,

a faint frown creasing his forehead. "And otherwise everything went okay?"

"Yes." Heather sensed an undertone to his question and thought of what John had told her about her father's implied warning.

"And now you're going riding?"

"If that's okay?"

"Of course it is. Just make sure that…that you're careful." He held her eyes a beat.

Heather paused a moment, feeling like a little girl again, waiting for some punishment to be meted out.

"Oh, Monty, don't be such a father. She'll be fine, won't you, Heather?" her mother asked with a bright smile. "Don't want to keep John waiting." She gave her a wink, and Heather sensed that her parents had a fair idea of what had happened while they were gone.

Trouble was, while her mom seemed perfectly happy about it, she sensed her father was not.

"Everything good?"

John stopped by the stall as Heather tightened the cinch of her saddle, then lowered her stirrups, her face turned away from him. When she'd joined them at the corrals she had seemed uptight. For a moment he'd thought she was coming to tell them that she wasn't joining them, but then she had gotten her tack out of the shed and taken it to where Rowdy was tied.

"Just fine," Heather said, stroking Rowdy's mane as she checked his headstall. She flashed John a smile, but then looked away.

He was fairly sure that her reserve had everything to do with meeting Sandy's parents in town. He and

Heather were moving toward something. And he didn't want to lose what was growing between them. Didn't want anything to jeopardize it.

So he took a chance and caught her by the arm. "Whatever Kim might have said, it doesn't matter," he stated quietly.

Heather's features softened. Her smile gave him hope.

"Thanks," she whispered.

He moved a bit closer and stroked her cheek with his finger. "I'm glad you came," he said. "I'm looking forward to this ride."

When she returned his smile, he felt a settling in his soul. He had to trust that God had brought Heather back into his life for a reason. That the feelings that he knew were growing between them would go somewhere.

He also had to believe that Monty would agree to take him on as a partner. Her dad had to know that John could take care of Heather and provide a future for her and Adana.

He pushed the nagging thoughts aside. For now they were going for their first ride out into the hills, and he was determined to enjoy it.

He walked over to his horse, Clyde, checked the cinch once more, then climbed into the saddle.

Tanner and Keira went ahead and John let his horse lag until Heather and Rowdy caught up. They rode side by side in companionable silence, the warmth of the sun and the gentle plodding of the horses' hooves on grass still soft from the snowmelt creating a soothing rhythm. Whenever John glanced at Heather, he saw a look of peace and contentment on her face.

"I missed this so much," she said as they made their way across the pasture toward the hills behind the ranch house. Rowdy shook his head, his bridle clanking, and she reached out to stroke his neck.

"Don't imagine you had much chance to go riding in New York," John teased.

"Sometimes I would go to Central Park and pet the horses there," she said, giving him a shy smile. "Talk to the hansom cab drivers. Horse talk."

"Mitch ever go with you?"

Heather grew silent. Her peaceful expression faded and John felt like kicking himself. Why did he seem to have this obsessive need to find out about her and Mitch?

"I'm sorry," he said. "I didn't mean to make you upset."

Heather shook her head. "No. You didn't. Not really." She looked away a moment, as if gathering her thoughts, then her gaze returned to him. "I don't like talking about Mitch because I've been trying to forget that time. I'm not…not proud of that part of my life…"

Again she hesitated and again John had to stifle a flicker of curiosity. What had happened to her while she was married to Mitch?

"I don't really want to talk about him," she said. "Not yet."

It was the "yet" that sparked hope. The imperceptible promise of other confidences and a deepening relationship.

"We can talk about Adana, if you prefer."

"She's such a sweetheart," Heather said, her grin restoring his good spirits. "She certainly has a way of working herself into someone's heart."

"She does. In spite of how hard it was after she was born, what I had lost, holding her created a fierce love that surprised me."

Heather turned to him, the spring breeze tossing her hair around her face. "You must have had such mixed emotions, taking her home and leaving Sandy behind."

John nodded slowly, thinking back to those difficult months after Sandy's death. In spite of the passage of time, he felt his throat thicken. He blinked away tears, then Heather moved Rowdy closer to Clyde and stroked John's shoulder.

"Again, I'm so sorry. Sandy was such a good person. She should have been able to hold her baby. To see Adana growing up." To his surprise, Heather's voice broke and her grasp tightened on his shoulder. "I wish I could say the right thing. Do the right thing."

"You already have," he said. He caught her hand and squeezed it, then his horse moved away from hers and their hands were pulled apart. But the moment had helped bring them closer together.

"Hey, you two, this was supposed to be a ride," Keira called back to them, turning to grasp the cantle of her saddle. "Not some sedate stroll in the pasture."

Heather gave John a quick smile, then pulled her hat lower on her head.

"I'll take that challenge," she cried to her sister. She nudged Rowdy and he broke into a canter, then a gallop.

John held his horse back, appreciating the sight of Heather riding ahead of him, her hair flying, her movements easy, fluid, in tune with her horse.

This was the real Heather, he thought with a sense of satisfaction as he nudged his own horse into a canter. This was the Heather he remembered and had loved.

Though memories of Sandy lingered, he thought she would have approved of him moving on with his life.

And in that moment John knew exactly what it was he wanted and what he needed to do.

This was freedom, Heather thought—having wind in her face and Rowdy's hooves beating out a happy rhythm. Pure, unadulterated freedom.

Exhilaration hummed through her as the ground sped past, Rowdy's hooves tossing up huge clumps of dirt behind her. The Montana sunshine beat down on her, the wind snapped her hair away from her face and in spite of the speed, she was in control.

She raced down the pasture along the fence, feeling as if she was shedding the last fragments of her past. As if Rowdy's speed and the wind whistling past her were brushing away the memories.

But as she rode, she saw they were getting closer to the gates leading to the upper pastures.

Reluctantly, she pulled back on the reins, slowing Rowdy to a canter. The horse shook his head, showing his reluctance to stop, but Heather stayed firm and he moved from the canter into a trot.

Posting in time to his movements, Heather slowly

brought him to a full stop. She leaned back in the saddle, taking a minute to catch her breath and enjoy the utter peace of the moment. The breeze dancing through the trees and the faint chirping of warblers and sparrows were the only sounds in the stillness of the day. She turned Rowdy toward the others, catching snatches of conversation as they crested a hill, heading toward her.

John waved to her, then nudged his horse closer. Rowdy's ears pricked up and his head lifted.

"You look flushed," John said when he joined her, his own horse breathing hard. "Out of shape?"

"Maybe a bit, but so excited and happy." She gave him a wide smile, her heart full. "I haven't felt that free for years."

He leaned back in his saddle, resting his hands on the cantle as he glanced over the field. "That's all well and good, but it seems you've made some divots in the hay field," he teased.

"I'll replace them," she said, still smiling. "But I'm sure by the time the cows get out here you won't even see the evidence of my race with the wind." She pulled her hat off, ran her hands through the tangle that was her hair, and dropped her hat back on. "But I'm happy to find out that even after all these years, Rowdy's still got it," she said, reaching down to rub his heaving sides. He snorted, shifting his feet. "You want to go again, buddy?" she asked him, smoothing his tousled mane. "You miss racing?"

"The real question is, do you?" John asked.

Heather shook her head. "I don't miss running around from rodeo to rodeo, but sometimes I miss the exhilaration of competing," she said, gathering up the reins. "I enjoyed pushing myself, pushing Rowdy, trying to see how close I could cut the barrels, how quick I could make the turnaround."

"You were good at it. I was always surprised you didn't take it further."

Heather shrugged, trying not to let regret take over. "I might have, if Mom and Dad hadn't pushed me to go to college."

"You know, when I see you riding, I feel like I see the real Heather," John murmured.

"What do you mean?"

"I see a smile on your face now that wasn't there when you first came home."

"There's other reasons," Heather stated with a coy grin.

"I'm glad for that," he said. He took her hand, and pressed a gentle kiss on the back of it. "You are precious to me, you know."

His words spilled over the dark places of her life like a waterfall. She curled her hand around his cheek. "Thanks," she said.

"You have your own specific strengths and talents. I think you should find a way to use them."

"Like doing that clinic your mom was talking about?"

"It's a thought. There's also a growing demand for trained barrel-racing horses. That could be another possibility."

Heather felt as if God was gently pointing her in a different direction than she'd been heading when she'd come here. Ever since she had heard about the job from John's mother, the idea had lingered in her mind.

"I think I would love the work. I just don't know if it would pay enough."

"That's important to you?"

"I need to be able to take care of myself," she said. She wanted to be a survivor. Not a victim, as she'd been in New York.

"I'd like to think I can help you there," he said quietly.

The import of his words hung heavy between them. Her heart fluttered, moved by his offer. Did she dare accept what she thought he was suggesting? It would mean changing her plans. Securing her future with his.

Would she be able to do that? Would he be willing, once he found out everything? She knew eventually she would have to tell him all the sordid details of her life. She wasn't sure she was ready for that yet.

"What's wrong?" John asked.

Confusion rushed through her, even as she looked at him. He had always been so important to her, and now, as they spent time together, as he was slowly weaving his way into her life again, she knew that leaving would be difficult. She wouldn't leave with her heart intact.

She looked at him, wondering what she dared tell him. Wondering how she could. "Let me think about it," she whispered, pulling away.

His eyes seemed to pierce her soul, as if trying to see what she was holding back from him.

She heard her sister call out, and glanced up as Keira and Tanner drew closer.

"You're looking very somber," Keira said. "Rowdy not performing up to his usual standards?"

"He's faster than your old nag," Heather retorted, jumping at the chance to tease her sister and focus on something else.

"You'd like to think so," Keira declared. Then she dug her heels into her horse and took off. Heather, never one to turn down a challenge, nudged Rowdy in the flanks. It was all the encouragement he needed. In ten strides they had caught up to Keira. Four more and they were past them.

And Heather let the troubles that clung to her brush away with the wind that blew over her face.

She would deal with them another time. For now, she was free.

Chapter Twelve

"I have to say, I'm feeling a bit overwhelmed right now." Keira stood at the table in the church hall, looking around the festively decorated room, full of women who had come out for her bridal shower. Green and yellow paper puffs hung from the ceiling and mini lights sparkled from some trees that Heather and Monty had placed in buckets. A pile of gifts, now unwrapped, spilled over a table beside them. All a harbinger of the wedding that would take place in early summer.

Heather smoothed out a wrinkle in her dress, glancing around at all the ladies from her seat beside Keira. Many of the faces were familiar, a few were new. All were smiling as Keira spoke.

"I'm so thankful for the support of the community and I'm so thankful for all the lovely gifts." Keira paused and Heather caught a surprising shimmer in her eyes. "It's overwhelming and I'm thankful that God has brought us all here together. Living here is a real blessing, both to me and to Tanner." Keira turned to Heather and placed her hand on her shoulder. "I also want to thank Heather, as well as my friend Brooke, for helping Mom with the shower. It means a lot to have my sister here beside me." Her hand tightened on Heather's shoulder.

"And I want to extend an invitation to all of you to come visit Tanner and me at our home, once we have it all set up after the wedding."

After a round of applause followed her comments, Keira sat down again, slowly exhaling, as if she'd been holding her breath the entire time.

"You okay?" Heather asked.

"Just glad the speech is done." Keira took a sip of her coffee. "But I was glad to have you beside me. You did such a great job with the baking and the decorating. Thanks again." She beamed as she looked around the hall once more. "It looks so beautiful."

"I enjoyed doing it and I would gladly do it again."

Heather had been working until late last night, baking and frosting cookies and squares. This afternoon she, Monty and John had met Brooke at the hall, and they had decorated and gotten most of the food set up. It was worth it to see Keira's look of surprise and delight when she'd seen the place.

And it had been even more worth it when John had caught her in a corner of the kitchen and stolen a few kisses.

"You might have to help me come up with some ideas for decorating the hall for the wedding," Keira said. "I'm still not sure what I want to do."

"Really? I can't imagine that," Brooke chimed in from her seat across the table. She closed the notebook she'd been writing in, noting gifts and the names of their givers for thank-you cards. "I think I've had my wedding planned since I was a little girl."

"And I see from your Pinterest account that you're still going with the pink-and-black theme," Heather teased.

"It's very hip again," Brooke returned with a grin. "What about you? You still have your dream wedding planned? I seem to remember peach being a favorite color."

"Been there, done that," Heather said, thinking back to the hastily put together wedding to Mitch. Monty, Ellen and Mitch's mother had been the only family members in attendance. Heather had preferred it that way.

"I'm sorry," Brooke said with a lopsided smile. "I wasn't thinking."

Heather held up her hand to dismiss her concerns. "Don't worry about it, sweetie. I don't know if another wedding is in my future." She caught Keira's raised eyebrows and knew her sister was thinking about her and John.

Her hand touched her lips as if to feel the kiss John had given her only a few hours ago.

"I think it might be a strong possibility," Keira said with a mischievous grin.

"Really? What's going on?" Brooke leaned forward, her eyes bright with anticipation. "Is it John? Are you two back together again? I saw how he looked at you today."

"Right now, the focus is Keira and her upcoming wedding," Heather said, putting the brakes on that train of thought. "We're not talking about peach-themed weddings."

"Who's having a peach-themed wedding?" Marnie Giesbrook stopped by the table, her jean jacket slung over her shoulder. Marnie and her husband, Seth, ran the Feed and Seed, and as long as Heather could remember she had never seen Marnie in anything but plaid shirts and blue jeans. "I thought you were going with green and yellow?" she said to Keira.

"It's nothing. Just girl talk," Heather's sister replied.

"Girl talk about a certain George Bamford?" Marnie said with an exaggerated wink Brooke's way. Brooke's attraction to the laconic owner of the Grill and Chill was no secret, but Brooke blushed, anyway.

"We're not talking about George anymore," she said, looking down at the notebook she had been writing in.

"She's done with him right now," Keira said in an exaggerated whisper.

Marnie's loud bark of laughter echoed through the hall, catching a few people's attention. "I'm sure that will change the next time he pours you an extra cup of coffee without you asking," she said, patting her on the shoulder.

Brooke gave her a wan smile, then got up, beckoning to Keira. "I need to go over the list of gifts with you."

When they walked away, Marnie turned to Heather. "I hear that you might be sticking around?"

"Who did you hear that from?" she asked, puzzled.

She hadn't been in town much, other than the day she and John had seen his and Sandy's parents.

"Paige Argall told me."

"John's mom told you that?"

"She might have said that she was hoping you would stick around." Marnie winked.

Heather couldn't help grabbing a quick glance across the hall to where Paige stood, talking with Laura McCauley, the church's organist. The second-hand comment nurtured a glimmer of hope that John's parents wouldn't be completely against John and her getting back together.

"Anyhow, based on that, I thought I would talk to you about a couple of riding clinics I want to start up," Marnie was saying. "There's lots of girls who've been asking for 'em, but I don't have near the experience or expertise you do. I could have it at our arena. I know Seth's brother in Missoula was asking me about setting up some clinics around the state, too. You could be involved in that, as well. Pay isn't as much as you'd make modeling, but you could take on private clients, too. If you had a place to work with them, mind you."

Heather weighed Marnie's words carefully. It was as if pieces of her life were suddenly fitting into place.

It seemed too good to be true. Working at what she had always loved and staying in Saddlebank.

"I'll think about it," she said. Marnie gave her a quick nod, then left.

Heather noticed that one of the platters on the serving table was empty, and got up to fill it just as John's mother joined her at her table, Kim Panko right behind her.

"What do you think about Marnie's idea?" Paige said. "I know she has some good connections in the horse business. It could work out really well for you."

"It sounds great," Heather agreed. "I know I would love the work."

"Really?" Kim asked with a questioning lift of her eyebrow. "I can't see you working with horses and young girls anymore. You seem more the city type now."

Heather glanced down at the high heels, skinny jeans and chiffon top she had worn to the shower. Sure, her outfit looked more like it belonged in an upscale Fifth Avenue showroom, but it wasn't an indicator of who she really was.

"Looks can be deceiving," she murmured.

"I think you look lovely," Paige said with an encouraging smile. "And I think you should seriously consider Marnie's offer." She held Heather's eyes for a beat. "It would be lovely to have you back in Saddlebank."

Heather's heart jumped as the implications of what Paige was saying set in. As if she was giving her and John her blessing.

"Thank you," she said. "That means more than you can know."

Paige gave her a slow nod, then looked past her as Heather's mother joined them. "Ellen, this was a lovely shower. You must be so pleased."

Heather's mom slipped her arm around Heather's waist and gave her a gentle hug. "I am. Heather did an amazing job with all of this."

"She's an amazing girl," Paige said. "She has a

good eye. I remember that time she helped me paint my bedroom. I think you picked out the colors." Paige turned to her. "They were so cheerful."

"Or very bold," Kim said.

"I thought it looked nice," Ellen interjected.

"Russ certainly thought so, which surprised me. I thought he wouldn't like them." Paige gave her another smile. "But once he found out you had picked them, he thought they were beautiful. Of course, Russ always had a tender spot for you."

"Excuse, me, Paige, I think we should get going," Kim said.

"Sorry, Kim. Just reminiscing. But you're right." Paige gave Heather a quick hug. "So good to see you again. I'm so glad…" She paused, then shook her head, her smile widening. "Never mind. I'm just glad you're back."

But as she patted her gently on the cheek, Heather couldn't help wondering what she had been going to say.

"Thanks for everything," Kim said to Ellen as she slipped her coat on. Her eyes flicked to Heather, then away. "I've been trying to contact John, but he hasn't returned my calls today. I was hoping that I could come to the ranch and pick up Adana. We missed her a lot while we were gone, and would love to keep her for a couple of days. Maybe you could tell him to let me know if that works?"

Ellen nodded. "Of course. I'll get him to call you."

"Thank you so much. I truly appreciate that. And I want you to know that I'm praying for you. Praying that you will recover soon."

"Thank you so much, Kim. That is so kind of you."

Kim smiled at her, then glanced again at Heather, her smile fading just a bit. As she walked away, Heather couldn't rid herself of the notion that the woman's attitude toward her hadn't changed and probably wouldn't. It shouldn't matter to her, she told herself, and yet it did. Kim was Adana's grandmother, and Adana was John's daughter. And John was becoming more and more important in Heather's life.

More people started leaving, each saying their goodbyes, many of them telling Heather how happy they were to see her. The warm welcome eased away the feelings Kim Panko's veiled disapproval had created.

Half an hour later, the last person had finally left and Monty had arrived to help take decorations down. The gifts were packed away in the cars and the kitchen was cleaned up.

"I think we got everything," Heather announced, setting the last container of leftover blondies in the back of Keira's car.

"Let's go, then," her sister said, turning the key.

Heather climbed in, closed the door and let out a loud sigh.

"You sound tired," Keira commented, as she pulled out of the church parking lot.

"No, no. It was fun and I am so glad I could help out. It's just…" Her thoughts shifted back to Kim. "I'm never very comfortable around Mrs. Panko. I don't think she liked me much when I was friends with Sandy, and that hasn't changed."

"She's had a tough couple of years. Losing Sandy

really took a lot out of her. After all, she was their only child."

"I know that and I feel bad for her. I know I should have at least written to her when Sandy died, but I just didn't think she would appreciate it."

"It's hard to lose a child. But she has a strong faith and the support of a community. She'll get through it."

"I hope so," Heather said. Keira turned at the grocery store, taking a different route out of town. Heather felt her stomach drop as they passed a too-familiar street.

"Stop a minute," she said, touching Keira's arm. "Do you mind driving down this way?"

Her sister frowned, then slowed and turned onto the street Heather pointed out. They drove past a number of well-tended yards and houses, then past an empty field that still had some leftover hay bales lying out. Then the road went down toward the river and took a turn, and they ended up at a trailer park.

"Wait, isn't this—"

"Where I lived before I came to the ranch," Heather said, looking around at the trailers. "I haven't seen it since I left. Never had any reason to come down here."

"And Mom and Dad would never have let you."

"Funny that I never visited my mother after I was adopted. She never asked to see me. Never asked for a visit."

"Not the best mother, was she?"

Heather nodded. "I used to feel guilty that I didn't miss her more when I moved to the ranch."

"What was there to miss?" Keira asked. "She wasn't a good person to you."

Heather acknowledged her, then looked away from a place she had spent such a short time. "Thanks. I think I just needed a reminder."

"Of what?"

"Of where I came from. Let's get out of here."

Keira made a quick U-turn, then drove away. Heather gazed ahead, feeling as if she had put that part of her past behind her.

"So, I think the shower went well," she said as they made the final turn onto the highway and headed back to the ranch.

Keira beamed from ear to ear. "It was a wonderful day. I'm so thankful for all you did," she said. "Thanks again."

"Glad to help."

"Maybe someday I can do the same for you?"

The question hung between them, and Heather felt a flash of hope. Of possibilities.

"Maybe," she said softly.

"I get the idea that things between you and John are coming to a good place."

Heather thought of the moments they had shared the past few days and she wondered if she dared to change her plans for her future.

"They are. I think."

"So what's the problem?"

Heather rocked a bit in her seat, then finally released some of the misgivings that had been haunting her. "The problem is I don't know if I can do this. I don't have a history of making good choices. I've made mistakes that I regret. I've done things I regret. Sometimes I think I'm just like my mother."

"You are *nothing* like your mother," Keira snapped. "*Nothing*. You are loving and kind and caring. You're a good person. And the mistakes you made were when you were young and frightened."

"I know. But I still…"

"I'm pretty sure you've learned from your mistakes, and I'm sure John doesn't hold that against you," Keira continued. "You and he were meant to be together. I know that in my heart."

"Thanks for the encouragement," Heather said, giving her sister a thankful smile. "I just want to know that I can do this."

"What do you mean?"

Heather was surprised that it was so hard to talk to her sister about this. "I'm nervous. About opening myself up to someone again."

"Have you told John everything about Mitch?"

"What do you mean?"

Keira gave her a wry glance. "You know what I mean. About how Mitch treated you."

Heather automatically felt for the scar at her hip, as if reminding herself what he had done. "No."

"Are you ashamed? I know that's why I didn't tell Tanner about David. I thought I had brought it on myself."

"That's part of it," she said briefly.

"Part of it?"

Heather looked ahead of her, at the road winding across the open fields, the space flowing toward the mountains that she had been so taken with the first time she and her mother had moved to Saddlebank. She remembered praying to a God she had only a nodding acquaintance with, thanks to one summer living beside a church, and Vacation Bible School where her mother had sent her to get her out of her hair. Heather had prayed that she would be able to stay here in this beautiful place.

For a moment she realized that that fragile, half-formed prayer had been answered. At least for a part of her life.

And now? Would she be able to stay?

"Yes," It was all she could say.

"So there's more," Keira prodded.

"Yes."

"And you're not going to tell me?" Her question was a gentle probing rather than a demand.

"I can't. Not yet."

Keira reached over and caught her hand. "You don't have to tell me, but if you really want this to work with John, there is going to come a point where you have to open up and give him the whole truth. Trust me on this."

Heather nodded, knowing her sister was right. But at the same time, the shame she felt was too hard to leave behind. She wanted to be a survivor, not a victim. She didn't want to live in the past and she didn't want it to define her.

But she also knew that if she did delve too deeply into her past, she would open herself up to her biggest fear.

That she was just like her mother, after all.

* * *

John set Adana's suitcase on the floor of her bedroom. All packed up. His mother-in-law had called half an hour ago, asking if Adana could spend the night. He'd reluctantly agreed. Though they had done this a number of times in the past, he still found it difficult to let her go.

He went to his own bedroom, pulled a fresh shirt off the hanger and slipped it on. He had gone to his house after feeding the cows to change before going to the big house. He'd been invited for lunch. Not a hard invitation to accept if it meant seeing Heather again.

But what also got his pulse racing was the fact that Monty had said he had something important to tell him, and it couldn't wait.

Was he going to talk about the proposal for the ranch? John felt a twist of nerves in his stomach as he walked from the bedroom. Was Monty going to agree?

So much depended on a favorable outcome. John knew his relationship with Heather was getting serious. He'd been making plans and he hoped to talk to Heather about them soon.

But first he wanted to hear what Monty thought about the proposal. He wanted things settled before he moved to the next step.

He pulled his hat off the hook, glancing around his home, trying to imagine Heather living in it. Then came the realization that Sandy had never lived here. Hadn't heard Adana make her first noises here. Hadn't seen that first smile, those first steps.

Sandy never wanted to, he reminded himself. She had loved her job in Great Falls. Loved her work as an engineer, and had been glad to leave Saddlebank.

Yet, as he thought of Heather working in the kitchen, doing the baking and cooking that he knew she loved, it seemed right. It fit.

A knock on the door pulled him out of his daydreams. He dropped his hat on his head and pulled the door open.

Only to see Heather standing there, hands clasped in front of her, smiling.

The sun burnished her long blond hair, casting her face into intriguing shadows.

He pulled her close and kissed her. She melted against him for a moment, her arms slipping around him, responding to his kiss. Then she reluctantly drew away. "That's…that's not why I came here," she said, her voice breathless.

"Really?" John grinned down at her. "Then why did you kiss me back?"

"Habit," she retorted with a mischievous grin. "Actually, I came to get another outfit for Adana. She made a mess of the one you packed in her diaper bag this morning."

"Come on in, I'll help you pick something out." He walked toward Adana's room, Heather trailing along behind him. "I'm a little short. I packed a few clothes for her already," he said as he tugged a T-shirt off a hanger, followed by some leggings. "I don't know if I told you, but Sandy's mom is coming to pick her up this morning sometime."

Heather didn't reply. He turned to tell her again,

and caught her standing in the middle of the room, her arms wrapped around herself as she gazed at the crib with troubled eyes.

"You okay?" he asked.

"I had exactly the same one for…" Her voice drifted off as she ran her hand over the rails of Adana's bed.

John's heart sank.

"I'm so sorry." He closed the distance between them and gently drew her into his arms.

"It's just something I have to deal with," she said. "Something that comes with a lot of baggage."

"What kind of baggage?" he asked, wondering why she was suddenly so stiff in his arms.

"Nothing. It's okay." She gave him a tight smile, then stepped out of his embrace. John tried not to give in to the feeling that something else was going on.

He thought back to the moment when they were riding. How he'd sensed that she was holding something back from him. Uneasy questions sliced through his mind. Questions he didn't dare voice aloud.

He wanted to brush them off, but even as he looked at Heather's troubled face, he sensed that he would need the answers at some point if they were to move on with the relationship. He just wished he had a clue what it was.

"Okay. Then let's go have lunch." He walked out of the bedroom, trying to stifle the misgivings that had been hovering since their ride in the pasture. It seemed the closer they got in some ways, the farther apart they got in others.

Help me to trust You, Lord, he prayed as they

walked toward the house side by side, but not holding hands. *Help me to put this relationship into Your hands.*

He glanced at Heather, but she was looking directly ahead, biting her lip. Never a good sign.

"Something on your mind?" he asked, figuring it was worth a try.

"I'm thinking I might find a way to get to town this afternoon to talk to Marnie about running some clinics."

John stopped and caught her by the shoulder, the implications of her comment hitting him like a brick. "What? Really?"

"Yeah, really. The pay isn't as good as the job I was thinking of interviewing for in Atlanta, but I'm sure I'll manage. I know I'll enjoy it more. And…it means I can stay here."

His eyes held hers as his hand caressed her neck. "That would be the best part."

"Anyhow, just thought I would let you know," she said, gently pulling away.

"I'm glad you did." He grinned and, thankfully, she returned his smile.

She seemed jumpy, anxious, and John couldn't understand why. But that would have to wait. Maybe tonight they would have a chance to talk. Maybe they would have a reason to celebrate, depending on whatever Monty had to say to him.

Adana was already sitting in her high chair by the dining room table when they stepped into the house, so John just set her clean clothes on the kitchen counter.

"Smells good in here," he said as he walked over and brushed a quick kiss on his daughter's forehead.

"Heather made your favorite soup," Ellen said, setting a basket on the checkered tablecloth. "And cinnamon buns."

"Looks like a party," John said, eyeing the table, which was decorated with bouquets of pussy willows and spring blossoms.

"The flowers are leftover from the shower," Keira said, putting out a plate of cold cuts and tomato slices. "Seemed a shame not to use them."

"Lots of reasons to celebrate," Monty said as he walked from the living room. He had come from his study, John noticed, feeling a sudden onset of nerves.

Too many things going on at once, he thought, glancing from Monty to Heather. Too much riding on this moment.

"So, we're all here?" the rancher said, looking around as Keira hurried back to the stove to get the soup. The scent wafted past John, making his mouth water as she set it on the table. "Is Tanner coming?" Monty asked.

"No. He has work to do. We may be engaged but he's not exactly part of the family yet," Keira joked.

"And where does that put me?" John asked with a light laugh.

"You've always been part of this family," Ellen said as she carefully sat down, her neck brace making her movements stiff. She gave him a gentle smile that boded well for what he hoped Monty wanted to talk about. "Now, everyone sit," she commanded.

Keira dropped into the chair that had always been

her place at the table. John sat down on one side of Adana, Heather on the other.

"Let's pray," Monty said, glancing around the table. "Thank You, Lord, that we could be here together. Thank You for family and friends and for the food You've blessed us with. Thank You for spring and the promise it brings. New growth, new changes, new opportunities. Help us to use all of these gifts for You. Amen."

John held on to the prayer, thinking of the newness of his and Heather's relationship. And praying that they could find their way past old hurts to a future healing. He knew it was possible.

Monty picked up his napkin and spread it on his lap. Everyone started eating, chatting about the day. John tried not to let the tension overwhelm him. He knew he had to trust that God would bring him to the place he was supposed to be.

The conversation was easy and flowed from spring calving to Keira and Tanner's wedding to the ranch's upcoming 150th anniversary.

"I think we're getting an article done on the ranch by *Near and Far*, a travel magazine," Monty was saying. "I was approached by them when the editor found out about the anniversary."

"I heard Abby Newton works for that magazine," John said.

"She's not the one doing the piece." Monty frowned as he sliced his steak. "Someone named Burt Templeton will be."

"Good thing," Heather said. "I don't imagine Lee would be very comfortable around Abby."

"Thankfully we won't have to deal with that," Monty said, shooting a warning glance around the table. "Lee has served his time and paid his debt to society because of that accident. I'm just thankful he's coming back for the celebrations."

It wasn't too hard to hear the defensive tone in Monty's voice, so John kept his comments to himself. The accident that Lee had been involved in had sent him to jail and had put Abby's father in the hospital. It had also kept Lee away from the ranch for many years.

"I think it's wonderful that a magazine with such wide distribution is going to do a story on our ranch," Ellen commented. "We can be thankful for that."

"You're right," Monty said. "We have a lot to be thankful for. And right now I want to address one of the things I'm grateful for." He picked up his glass of water and raised it high. "I want to propose a toast to John and to the new partnership we are about to embark on. Welcome to Refuge Ranch, partner," he said, smiling across the table.

John felt his heart begin to race. He wanted to shout, grab Heather and spin her around. But he settled for a smile for Monty and allowing himself a silent prayer of thanks. Then he picked up his own glass and raised it.

"To Monty and Ellen and Refuge Ranch. Long may it produce and survive." He paused a moment, then turned to Heather, who was looking at him, her own bright smile easing away the misgivings he had felt a few moments ago. He wanted to say something to her, but not so publicly. Besides, he wanted to talk to Monty before he made any other commitment to Heather. Instead, he tilted his glass toward her. "To new beginnings," he said, trusting she knew what he meant.

Then John put his glass down, stood up and walked over to Monty, his hand held out.

"Thanks, Monty. I look forward to our partnership."

"I do, too." The rancher shook his hand. "I wish Lee could be here, but it is what it is."

John just nodded, acknowledging the momentary pain of Monty's son and heir not being around for this occasion. Of course, John knew part of the reason Monty had agreed to this partnership was because of Lee's absence. Nonetheless, he was thankful for the opportunity.

"All will be well," he said quietly, giving Monty's hand an extra squeeze.

The older man held his gaze for a long, meaningful moment, then his eyes shifted to Heather. "I think you're right. And I'm guessing that there might be other changes happening here?"

John felt a flush creep up his neck. Given the warning Monty had given him when Heather first arrived, he sensed her dad's reluctance had eased off.

John had hoped to talk to Monty privately, but at the same time he felt as if events were coming to a head. He looked over at Heather, thinking about her comment about accepting the job in Saddlebank. "We're taking it one step at a time," he said. "But I think we're moving in a good direction, Heather and I."

Monty nodded slowly. "That's good."

"This is so cool," Keira said, giving her sister an exuberant hug. "I'm so glad. After all Mitch put you through. All the pain and—" She stopped suddenly, clapping her hand over her mouth, her gaze shooting to John, then back to her sister. "I'm sorry," she said to Heather. "I wasn't thinking."

John frowned, wondering why Keira seemed so upset. It was no secret that Mitch had put Heather through a lot.

But when he caught Heather's horrified look at her sister and the quick shake of her head, his apprehension grew.

"Heather? What's going on?" he asked.

She gazed at him, eyes wide. He was about to ask her to talk to him outside when a knock on the back door interrupted the moment. The door opened and a voice called out, "Anybody home?"

It was Mrs. Panko, come to take Adana.

Talk about terrible timing.

Chapter Thirteen

Heather stared at John, her thoughts a jumble. She saw the question in his eyes, a question she didn't know if she was ready to answer. Half-formed thoughts spun through her mind as she tried to choose which one to formulate.

You have to tell him.

That's what Keira had said, and as Heather looked away from John, she caught her mother and father watching her with the same puzzlement.

But then Mrs. Panko stepped into the kitchen, the phone rang and Heather was given a momentary reprieve in the sudden influx of activity.

With shaking hands she picked up the phone. "Hello?"

"Can I talk to Heather, please," a male voice on the other end of the line said.

"This is Heather," she said, walking into the living room where it was quieter.

"It's Alan at the garage. Your car is ready to be picked up."

"Can you tell me what the bill is?"

"Hold on, let me check."

She clutched the phone, her heart beating wildly in her chest while she waited.

You have to tell him.

She knew that, but she wasn't ready to face John's reaction. Not when so many things were going on. He had just found out he would be a partner in the ranch. His life was finding a solid, steady place.

Herself?

She knew she wanted to stay in Saddlebank. She knew she wanted to be with John. She just didn't know what he would think if she told him everything.

"It comes to about twelve hundred dollars," the mechanic was saying.

That was less than half of what she had expected. "That's great. Can I pay you when I pick it up?"

"Has to be today by two o'clock. I'm closed after that and tomorrow."

"Okay. Thanks." She ended the call, feeling surprisingly carefree as she walked back to the dining room. Twelve hundred dollars was a lot, but that amount was manageable. Could things be truly changing for the better for her?

"That was the mechanic," she said, sitting down in her chair, giving John a quick smile. "My car is ready. I'm going to need a ride into town so I can pick it up before two."

"I can take you."

Mrs. Panko's unexpected statement startled Heather. She glanced over at her, puzzled as to why she would offer.

"I'm just here to pick up Adana," Kim said, jiggling her granddaughter on her lap. "I'm leaving right away. It seems a shame to take everyone else away from their work."

"It would save us the trip there and back," Monty said. "Besides, I want to go over a few things with you, John."

Heather felt a tiny bit of disappointment that John couldn't take her, but at the same time the option made sense.

"Okay. I guess that would work," she said. She wasn't too keen on spending half an hour in the car with Mrs. Panko, but it was the most practical solution.

"So, did you pack a bag for Adana?" Kim asked John.

"I'll get it," Heather answered, as she got up. She was glad for the few moments alone.

She found Adana's suitcase and picked it up. Just as she was about to leave, the door opened. She stopped when she saw John.

"I had to get some of my bank statements," he was saying. "It's for the partnership agreement."

"Of course." She smiled at him, her heart battering against her ribs. "Congratulations. I'm so glad that Dad agreed to take you on as a partner."

"It changes everything." John took a step closer. "It means I'm able to plan better for the future."

"That's good."

John remained silent, and Heather felt as if something had suddenly shifted. Not for the better.

"What did Keira mean?" he finally asked, his quiet

question increasing the pounding in Heather's chest. "What was she referring to when she talked about all the pain Mitch put you through?"

"I can't talk right now. Mrs. Panko is waiting and I just…I don't think…"

"There's something else going on. Something about Mitch that you're not telling me."

Heather looked at John but couldn't speak.

"If this is going to work between us, you have to talk to me," he pressed.

"I know. But I can't. Not yet." She pushed past him, carrying Adana's suitcase.

"When?" The anger in John's voice grew as he followed her down the hallway. "You have to tell me what's going on."

"I will. Soon," she said, each footstep seeming to emphasize the growing distance between them. She could feel John's frustration, but she couldn't deal with it yet.

"Don't run away from me," he insisted, catching up to her. "Don't shut me out again."

She felt a strong hand catch her arm and pull her around. Terror rushed through her, and she swung wildly, hitting his shoulder, pushing him away. "Stay away from me," she yelled, as she swayed on her feet.

Fear blended with anger coursed through her.

Heather pressed her lips together, clamping down the growing hysteria. She knew her reaction was way out of proportion to what John had done. It was instinctive. She was losing it in front of the only man she had ever loved.

John stood staring at her, eyes wide.

"It's me. John," he said quietly.

She took a few quick breaths, then nodded. "I know."

"I don't think you did a few moments ago."

Heather could only look at him, her past mingling with the present.

He stood in front of her, his hands clenched at his sides. "Please tell me what's going on."

She closed her eyes for a moment, feeling as if she was teetering on the edge of an abyss. One wrong step and she would fall.

"I need to know. If this is going to work, Heather, you have to tell me what that was all about. What is going on?"

She sent up a prayer for strength and courage.

"I don't know where to start." Heather willed her quavering voice to be strong.

"I think you should start with Mitch."

She bit her lip, inhaled a cleansing breath and began.

"Contrary to what you may think, Mitch and I never really dated when I left Saddlebank. He was just my manager," Heather said, setting the record straight at last. "At the same time, I knew he wanted to get back together with me. I didn't want that. I wanted to work and pay back Mom and Dad.

"I didn't make a lot of money at first. Catalog jobs didn't pay that much, or so I thought. Mitch handled my finances, which was a mistake, but I didn't really know any better. He had control of my life, though I wasn't aware of it at the time. Anyway, I started taking on other jobs, but didn't really like the work.

"When I found out about you and Sandy getting married, I realized that I would never get you back. I was upset one night. Mitch came. I talked about quitting modeling. He told me that would be an even bigger mistake. That I had a great future ahead of me. I was lonely and scared, and he stayed with me…"

Heather's voice faded away as shame overtook her. She cleared her throat and carried on. "I was pregnant a few months later. And I was upset. Mitch said we needed to get married. I didn't want to end up a single mom, like my mother, so I agreed. After a couple of months, I found out that he'd made some bad investments. And had lost most of my money. We fought about that, and that's when the abuse started."

"Abuse?"

Heather ignored John, unable to look him in the eye.

"He was careful," she said, keeping her voice even, emotionless, as she struggled with the shame and humiliation. "I still had a modeling contract. He told me to keep my pregnancy quiet. Otherwise I would lose work. Of course, he needed me to keep making money, but I also knew sooner or later it would become obvious. I was at a photo shoot one day for a magazine and I was joking with the photographer, and it came out that I was pregnant. Mitch heard us. That night he blew up." Heather's hand slipped, as it often did when she thought of that night, to the scar on her hip. The scar she got when Mitch pushed her so hard she fell down the stairs. "He beat me so badly, I lost the baby…" She faltered, feeling the pain, sorrow and shame coursing through her.

John's sudden intake of breath made her glance up. He looked horrified. Angry and disgusted.

"Why did you stay with him?"

"I didn't. Not after I lost the baby."

"But before that. Why didn't you leave before that? Why did you stay with him?"

Ice bloomed in Heather's chest, spreading to her hands and feet. She had bared her soul and made herself vulnerable, and *this* was John's reaction? She couldn't face it.

"Are you ready to go?" Mrs. Panko asked, stepping inside the house. She looked at Heather, then John, frowning as if she sensed she'd interrupted something.

Heather knew she should stay. Talk it through. But she couldn't. Her own emotions were rubbed raw. She needed to retreat. Regroup.

"Yes. I'm ready," she said. "Just let me get my purse."

"Heather," John called out, but she kept going. Later, she thought. She would deal with it later.

"Is everything all right?" Kim asked as they headed toward her car.

Heather guessed she was referring to the situation she had just walked in on.

"Yes. Everything is fine," she said, the lie coming automatically to her lips. It was her standard answer to Mitch whenever he sensed she was upset.

She tightened her grip on the handle of the suitcase as she reached the vehicle, which was parked by the house. Adana's car seat had already been moved from John's truck.

"I'll get Adana and meet you out here," Kim said.

Heather nodded, putting the suitcase in the trunk and then following her to the house to get her purse. Luckily, she usually left it on the porch. She didn't need to go inside to answer any awkward questions.

She caught a glimpse of her mother looking over at her as Kim lifted Adana out of the high chair. Heather gave her mom a quick smile and wave, then hurried out of the house.

Thankfully, Mrs. Panko was quick, and by the time she had Adana in her seat and had slid behind the wheel, John still hadn't come out of his house.

But as they drove away from the ranch, Heather saw him striding across the yard, clutching a large envelope. Probably the papers he'd been looking for.

Sorrow gripped her at the sight. What would happen to them now?

"So, that's happy news for John," Kim said. "Him becoming partners with Monty."

"I'm sure he's thrilled." Pain, as heavy and solid as a rock, settled in Heather's chest. His reaction to her news—his shock, his confusion, his retreat—all battered at her already fragile emotions. She didn't want to chitchat with Kim. Not as they drove away from the man who had so easily recaptured her heart. Heather wasn't sure how to interpret his reaction, but deep down, she knew it wasn't good.

"I'm thankful he found a good use for the insurance settlement he received when Sandy passed away," Kim was saying. "I know he felt guilty for getting it and wanted to give some to us, but we told him that he had to think of Adana and her future. I know we were hoping he would start up a business closer to town, but we can't complain. At least this way Adana is only half an hour away. We can still see her whenever we want, can't we, munchkin?"

Kim shot a glance in the rearview mirror at her granddaughter. The toddler's cheeks were red and she gave a huge yawn. Heather suspected she would be asleep before they got to the road.

"She's a cutie, isn't she?" Kim declared.

"She's adorable," Heather agreed, tired from the constant stream of talk.

"You sound like you've become attached to her."

"It wasn't too hard to become attached."

"I know for us, our connection to her is so strong because of losing Sandy."

"I'm sorry, again, for your loss," Heather said. "Sandy was a wonderful person. I owe her a lot. It was thanks to her that Ellen found out what was happening with my mom, and I got moved to the Bannister household."

"When was the last time you saw your mother?"

"It's been a while. I haven't been around much."

"I know." Kim's words had an edge that cut as sharply as any knife. "And when will you be leaving again?" she continued.

"Leaving?"

"Yes. You're going to Atlanta for your interview in a few days, aren't you?"

The assumption that she was leaving was more than Heather wanted to deal with right now. But she didn't have the energy or the ability to erect defenses.

"I don't know. I was going to go talk to Marnie

Giesbrook today about setting up barrel-racing clinics," she said.

"Would you be happy doing that? After working as a model?"

The faint disdain in Kim's voice cut, so Heather chose not to answer.

"I know this is hard for you. I know you loved John at one time, but I want you to consider…" Kim paused, biting her lip, as if unsure how to carry on. "I don't know how to phrase this more delicately, but I'd like you to consider keeping away from him. He's a good man. He loved our daughter dearly and I know he's still grieving Sandy's death. You have your own complicated history and, let's face it, you haven't had the best role model with your real mother. I know Ellen is a gem, but your more formative years were spent with your birth mother. And I got to see firsthand what she was like and how she behaved. We love Adana dearly and we want only what's best for her."

Kim Panko shot her words out like poisoned arrows. Heather found herself reeling from the precise verbal hits that only reinforced what she had just told John.

She couldn't protect her own baby, let alone take care of someone else's. She was just like her mother in more ways than one. In more ways than she wanted to admit.

Chapter Fourteen

"Hey, Marnie. Did Heather come to see you?" John clung to the phone, his other hand planted on his hip as he stood looking out the window of his house. He'd spent the past couple hours trying to track her down. When he'd first called her cell phone, Keira had answered, telling him that Heather had left it behind at the ranch.

He had called the mechanic. Heather had picked up her car before two. When John called Kim, all she'd told him was that she had dropped Heather off at the mechanic's and hadn't seen her since.

It was now four o'clock and she still wasn't back from town. As far as he knew, the only errands she'd planned were to get her car and talk to Marnie.

"No. I was hoping she would come today. I thought she was going to," Marnie said.

John leaned his forehead against the cool glass of the window. His head ached and his heart hurt.

He knew he had overreacted to Heather's news.

But what else was he supposed to do? She'd thrown all that information at him and then left.

She hadn't stuck around long enough for him to absorb what she'd told him. To deal with it and talk to her about it.

He started calling a few other numbers. Brooke hadn't seen Heather, nor had she stopped in at the Grill and Chill. She hadn't picked up groceries or visited any of the gas stations in town.

He finally put the phone down. He had no other choice. He was going to have to drive to town to find her. It was a long shot, but he didn't know what else to do.

He grabbed his jean jacket, settled his hat on his head and was about to leave when Keira came up the walk. His heart lifted. He yanked open the door just as she raised a hand to knock.

But the concerned look on her face told John that she didn't know anything, either.

"I don't suppose you've heard from Heather," he said, shoving his hands in the back pockets of his blue jeans.

Keira shook her head. "Can I come in?"

John stepped aside and let her enter. Maybe what she had to say would help him find Heather.

Keira looked around the house. "Heather always loved this place, you know," she said gently.

John stifled a moment of frustration, reminding himself just to listen.

"I'm worried about her," Keira said. "She's not back from town yet."

"I know. I was going to go out and look for her.

I'm afraid that I wasn't…wasn't helpful just before she left."

"What do you mean?"

John pushed his hat back on his head and sighed. "She told me about Mitch, how he treated her and how she lost the baby because of him, and I asked her why she'd stayed with him. It was a stupid thing to say."

Keira gasped, and John guessed it was her reaction to his unthinking question.

"Why do you think she did?" he asked. "I don't understand why she didn't come home. Why she let him do that to her."

Keira clasped her hands together, as if gathering her thoughts. "I don't know what Heather told you about her life with her mother, but it was incredibly rough. Hard on her. I remember she had a couple of bruises that were different colors, which meant one was newer than the older one. I wonder if she didn't think that the kind of life Mitch gave her was the only kind she deserved. He was like her mom, and maybe she felt that would be the pattern of her life. It's not unusual."

"I want to find her. Want to talk to her. I need to talk to her." John dragged a hand over his face, wishing he could sort out his thoughts. "This time around I don't want to let her get away, I want to fight for her. I want to show her what she really means to me, but I don't know where to start."

"I think I have an idea where you might find her," Keira said.

Heather sat on the hill overlooking the trailer park that had been her home for the six months she'd lived with her mother in Saddlebank.

The tin was peeling off the sides of the trailer she and her mom had lived in, and she could see the roof was lifting in places. The wooden steps leading to the door were askew, the handrail broken. Dried weeds choked what was supposed to be a lawn and flower beds.

She had already tried knocking on the door, but no one answered, and from what she could see through the broken window, it looked as if no one had lived there for a long while. As a young girl, she had never stayed in any one place longer than six or seven months, anyhow. But Kim's comment about her mother had sent her here to check for herself.

The sound of canned laughter from a television show drifted out a window of one of the trailers. A truck engine growled down the street and a few kids ran down the cracked sidewalk below her, laughing. Heather wrapped her hands around her knees, still looking at the trailer below her, trying to separate who she was now from who she'd been then. From her mother's memory.

See, I have engraved you on the palms of my hands.

The quote from the Bible passage floated over the past.

Heather clung to the words. She was valuable. She was important. Not because she was Heather, but because she was God's child.

She laid her head on her knees and drew in a long, steadying breath as she felt the connection to her mother loosen. She wasn't her mother's daughter. She was first and foremost God's child.

"Help me, Lord," she whispered. "Help me to know

who I am. To believe that You love me just as I am, but also that You will help me become better. That You will help me be the person You see me to be."

The sound of a vehicle stopping directly below her made her lift her head. She saw a dark truck that was achingly familiar. The same truck she had seen only a few weeks ago, when she'd come back to the area.

John got out, his eyes fixed on her.

He paused a moment, as if unsure what to do. Then he slammed the door of the truck and strode up the hill toward her.

"Keira told me you might be here," he said, pulling his hat off his head as he stopped near her.

Heather looked up at him, not certain what to think. Her eyes skittered away. She wasn't sure where to look.

Then John sat down beside her, facing the trailer, his wrists resting on his bent knees, his hat hanging from his fingers.

"So, is this where you lived when you and your mother moved here?" he finally asked.

"Until I got adopted by the Bannisters, yes." She had to stifle a sense of shame at the sight of the ramshackle trailer.

John was quiet a moment, working his hat around in his hands, then he turned to her. "I don't really know what to say, so I'll go with I'm sorry. I shouldn't have reacted the way I did. All I can say, in my defense, is that I was shocked. Shocked and angry." His hands tightened on his hat as his eyes held hers. "I wanted to hurt Mitch very badly."

Heather couldn't look away from him. "I thought you were disgusted with me."

"I was disgusted. But not with you. Never with you." He reached out to touch her, then pulled his hand away, as if he had no right. "Never with you. With Mitch and what he did to you. You have to believe me."

"I want to," she said, a lifetime of insecurity edging around her subconscious. "It's just that I've struggled so long with the thought that I'm like my mother. I figured that what happened with me and Mitch made me just like her."

"How can you say that? You are nothing like your mother."

His words, the exact replica of what Keira had said as they drove away from the bridal shower, gave Heather renewed hope. And the fierceness of his tone awoke the possibilities she had quashed on her drive with Mrs. Panko.

"How do you know?" she asked, as if testing what he was telling her, to see if it would hold under questioning. He was silent for a moment, letting her inquiry fade away in the quiet afternoon air. But behind that question hovered Mrs. Panko's comments, which so easily underlined the misgivings that had always haunted Heather. "I've made so many of the same bad decisions she made."

"I don't remember ever seeing your mother after you moved in with the Bannisters. Was she allowed to visit?"

"I think so."

"Did your mother ever call you after you moved to the ranch?"

Heather slowly shook her head, wondering where he was going. "No. She didn't."

John gave her a careful smile, lifted his hand as if to touch her, then stopped. Heather wished he would, but waited, sensing he had more to say.

He turned his hat around in his hands. "The reason I can say with such conviction that you are nothing like your mother is because I saw the sorrow in your face when you looked at Adana. I saw how it hurt you to be around her. I know now that you were still grieving the child you lost. I know, if you had an inkling that she was still alive, you would move heaven and earth to find her. Something your mother never did."

"But some of the choices I made…"

"You made those choices because you were scared. Because I didn't listen to you. Not because you are like her, but because you didn't get the support you should have." He reached out and touched her face gently, his finger grazing her cheek, his eyes expressing the regret she heard in his voice. "I'm so sorry I wasn't there for you."

"You, of all people, have nothing to be sorry for," she said softly.

"You're wrong. I do. I'm sorry I didn't listen better to you when you called me from college, when you were so lost and confused. I'm sorry I didn't get into my truck and drive down and talk to you face-to-face instead of thinking you were trying to break up with me."

"Which I did."

"Because I didn't fight for you like Monty and Ellen did." John cupped her face in his hand. "You were scared and alone, and I left you there. You may have been the one to make the first move, but I pushed you to do it. I should have known better and should have trusted you more."

His words were like a balm and Heather let them heal her.

"I care for you more than I thought it was possible to care for anyone," he continued, his voice growing quiet. He put his hand on her shoulder, his palm heavy, strong and warm. "I...I love you."

Heather gasped as she looked up at him, hardly daring to believe what he was saying.

"I love you, Heather. I think I always have. I know I always will."

She could only stare at him.

He released a nervous laugh. "So I'm thinking this isn't what you want to hear?"

"It is. It is something I've been waiting to hear all my life."

She pulled him close, pressed her lips to his and he wrapped his arms around her, creating a place of safety and security.

She let his touch comfort and strengthen her.

After a long, satisfying moment, he tucked her head against his neck, his cheek pressed against hers as he eased out a deep sigh. "It's been a long time getting here," he said, gently rocking her. "But I'm so thankful we made it. I never want you to leave. I need you to stay. I want you to be my wife."

Heather closed her eyes, reveling in the moment.

Then she gently pulled away and brushed a kiss over his cheek. Bracketing his beloved face between her hands, she held his gaze.

"I want to be your wife," she said. "I want you to be my husband. I'd love to be a mother to Adana. I'm going to need your help, though."

John shook his head, brushing a strand of hair out of her face, and following up with another kiss. "No. You won't need any help at all. You know exactly how to be a mother."

"You think so?"

"I know so." He took her hand and squeezed it tightly. "You have a loving heart. I think we'll do just fine."

"With God's help and guidance, I think we will, too."

He kissed her again as if to seal their declarations.

"Can we get up now?" he asked.

"Of course."

"The grass is still a bit wet," he said, standing and pulling her to her feet.

"I know. I didn't want to say anything to spoil the moment."

John laughed. "I don't think anything can spoil this moment. Now let's get back to the ranch."

"Back home," Heather said.

"I love the sound of those words," he replied, punctuating that with another kiss.

Epilogue

"I think the Pankos are here," John called out from the porch.

Heather ran her hands down her jeans, surprised at how nervous she was about facing Sandy's parents again. Especially Kim.

After Heather and John had expressed their love for each other, they had come back to the ranch house to talk to Monty and Ellen. John had asked Monty for his daughter's hand and, thankfully, her father had agreed.

They had spent some time together, laughing, planning and simply enjoying the moment.

Then John had called his mother-in-law and asked her to please bring Adana home tonight. Both Heather and John wanted her back at the ranch.

"It's fine," Ellen had said, touching Heather's shoulder. "You and John need to talk to her and straighten a few things out. She had no right to tell you what she did."

In spite of her mother's assurances that all would

go well with Kim and Rex, Heather's heart fluttered like a panicked bird. She inhaled a number of deep breaths, the same thing she did before every photo shoot. Then she sent up a quick prayer and walked through the kitchen to the porch, where John was pulling on his boots.

He stood and gave her a smile of assurance, pulling her into his arms and pressing a gentle kiss to her lips. "It will be fine," he said. "They're good people at heart."

Then, holding hands, they walked out to the car.

Rex had taken Adana out of her seat and Kim was walking around the vehicle, carrying her overnight bag. She stopped when she saw John and Heather.

Then she walked over to her husband and took Adana from him, holding her close.

"Thanks for bringing Adana back early," John said, stopping in front of his in-laws. "We wanted her to be here with us." He squeezed Heather's hand and pulled her closer. "I just asked Heather to marry me and she's agreed. We wanted Adana to be a part of this."

Kim's gaze flicked from Heather to John, then to Adana, and Heather caught the glint of tears in her eyes.

"I see," she said simply.

"Congratulations to both of you." Rex shook John's hand and gave Heather a nervous smile.

Rex had always been kind to her and Heather returned his smile. "Thank you so much."

Kim rested her head on Adana's, and Heather's

heart crumpled when she saw the tears drifting down the older woman's face.

She pressed a kiss to her granddaughter's cheek. "Go to Heather. She's going to be your new mommy now. I'll miss you so much." Kim closed her eyes, rocking the little girl. Rex rested his hand on Adana's shoulder and Heather saw the glint of tears in his eyes, as well.

"Never forget us, little girl," Rex said, his own voice gruff.

Heather glanced from Kim to Rex, confused. "You sound as if you might never see her again," she said in a questioning voice. "Why would you think that?"

Kim sniffed, then looked slowly up at her. "You're going to be John's wife. He has his parents, you have yours. That's hard enough to juggle as it is."

"But she's still your granddaughter," Heather said, stunned that they would think they would simply be shut out of Adana's life.

"That will never change," John reiterated.

Kim swiped her tears away one-handed, her cheeks still damp. "What do you mean?"

"Heather and I both know how important family is," John said, giving her a smile of encouragement. "Our marriage will change things for Adana. But you need to know that you will always have a place in her life that no one will ever take away."

Kim was speechless.

"Thanks so much for that," Rex said, slipping his arm around his wife and pulling her and his granddaughter close.

Kim looked down at Adana, fresh tears flowing. "That means so much to us," she said. Then she turned to Heather. "I have to admit, when you came back I was scared. I've always known how special you were to John." Kim held her gaze. "I was jealous of the place you held in his life, that was all. I wasn't a good person to you, and I was afraid that if you and John got back together again, you would push me out because of how I treated you, then and now."

Heather heard the pain in her voice and appreciated the woman's honesty. She laid a reassuring hand on her shoulder.

"I know from personal experience how hard life can be," she said. "I also know that you can't have too many people watching your back. I spent a lot of years without a father and with an absent mother. Adana is so blessed to have so many people who love her. I would appreciate and welcome your help in raising this little girl."

Kim released a short laugh. "I may not have always been approving of you, or welcoming, but I do know that you were a loving friend to my daughter. And I know you will be a good mother to Adana. You have a good, faithful heart."

"Hearing you say that means more than you will ever know," Heather murmured.

"Again, I'm so sorry," Kim said. Then she sighed, pressed another kiss to the little girl's head and started to hand her over to Heather. But Adana clung to her, snuggling into her shoulder.

"Honey, you need to go to Heather," Kim said.

"Wuv you, Gamma," Adana answered.

John put one hand on Kim's shoulder and held

Heather's with the other, as if completing a circle. "We're family. We need each other. That will never change."

"That's a real blessing," Rex said. "And we want to wish you God's richest blessing, as well."

Kim gave them both a teary smile. "I agree with Rex."

Then, together, they walked toward the ranch house. Toward their new future.

* * * * *

Dear Reader,

Every day of our life we are faced with choices. In *Reunited with the Cowboy*, Heather is dealing with the consequences of both her biological mother's choices and her own. The problem is, she is struggling with the idea that she has made the same poor choices her mother did, when in many ways she was simply surviving. We are all, to a point, products of our environment, but we are also products of our choices. The reality is that while we are making the decisions we do, we also have to realize that our lives are a work in progress. One choice will lead us in one direction. Another choice could take us on a different path. I believe that if we daily entrust our choices to God and try to work for His purpose, He will guide us and use the circumstances of our lives to work out His will and good work.

Blessings in the choices you make today.

Carolyne Aarsen

P.S. I love to hear from my readers. Drop a line to caarsen@xplornet.com or stop by my website at carolyneaarsen.com to find out about new and upcoming books. Sign up for my newsletter as well, to keep informed of the latest news.

REQUEST YOUR FREE BOOKS!

2 FREE INSPIRATIONAL NOVELS
PLUS 2
FREE
MYSTERY GIFTS

Love Inspired®

New York Times **bestselling author**

LINDA GOODNIGHT

**welcomes you to Honey Ridge, Tennessee,
and a house that's rich with secrets and brimming
with sweet possibilities.**

Memories of motherhood and marriage are fresh for Julia Presley—though tragedy took away both years ago. Finding comfort in the routine of running the Peach Orchard Inn, she lets the historic, mysterious place fill the voids of love and family. Life is calm, unchanging...until a stranger with a young boy and soul-deep secrets shows up in her Tennessee town.

Julia suspects there's more to Eli Donovan's past than his motherless son, Alex. But with the chance discovery of a dusty stack of love letters, the long-dead ghosts of a Civil War romance envelop Julia and Eli, connecting them to the inn's violent history and challenging them both to risk facing yesterday's darkness for a future bright with hope and healing.

New women's fiction from Linda Goodnight.
Please visit lindagoodnight.com for more information.

Pick up your copy today!

Be sure to connect with us at:
Harlequin.com/Newsletters
Facebook.com/HarlequinBooks
Twitter.com/HQNBooks

When the truth comes to light about Oregon Jeffries's daughter, will Duke Martin ever be the same again?

Read on for a sneak preview of
THE RANCHER TAKES A BRIDE,
the next book in
Brenda Minton's
miniseries **MARTIN'S CROSSING**.

"So, Oregon Jeffries. Tell me everything," Duke said.

"I think you know."

"Enlighten me."

"When I first came to Martin's Crossing, I thought you'd recognize me. But you didn't. I was just the mother of the girl who swept the porch of your diner. You didn't remember me." She shrugged, waiting for him to say something.

He shook his head. "I'm afraid to admit I have a few blank spots in my memory. You probably know that already."

"It's become clear since I got to town and you didn't recognize me."

"Or my daughter?"

His words froze her heart. Oregon trembled and she didn't want to be weak. Not today. Today she needed strength and the truth. Some people thought the truth could set her free. She worried it would only mean losing her daughter to this man who had already made himself

LIEXP0415

a hero to Lilly.

"She's my daughter." He repeated it again, his voice soft with wonder.

"Yes, she's your daughter," she whispered.

"Why didn't you try to contact me?" He sat down, stretching his long legs in front of him. "Did you think I wouldn't want to know?"

"I heard from friends that you had an alcohol problem. And then I found out you joined the army. Duke, I was used to my mother hooking up with men who were abusive and alcoholic. I didn't want that for my daughter."

"You should have told me," Duke stormed in a quiet voice. Looks could be deceiving. He looked like Goliath. But beneath his large exterior, he was good and kind.

"You've been in town over a year. You should have told me sooner," he repeated.

"Maybe I should have, but I needed to know you, to be sure about you before I put you in my daughter's life."

"You kept her from me," he said in a quieter voice.

"I was eighteen and alone and making stupid decisions. And now I'm a mom who has to make sure her daughter isn't going to be hurt."

He studied her for a few seconds. "Why did you change your mind and decide to bring her to Martin's Crossing?"

"I knew she needed you."

Don't miss
THE RANCHER TAKES A BRIDE
by Brenda Minton,
available May 2015 wherever
Love Inspired® books and ebooks are sold.